love the one you're with

Gossip Girl novels created by Cecily von Ziegesar:

Gossip Girl
You Know You Love Me
All I Want Is Everything
Because I'm Worth It
I Like It Like That
You're The One That I Want
Nobody Does It Better
Nothing Can Keep Us Together
Only In Your Dreams
Would I Lie To You
Don't You Forget About Me
It Had To Be You
The Carlyles
You Just Can't Get Enough
Take A Chance On Me
Love The One You're With

If you like gossip girl, you may also enjoy:

The **Poseur** series by Rachel Maude
The **Secrets of My Hollywood Life** series by Jen Calonita
Betwixt by Tara Bray Smith
Haters by Alisa Valdes-Rodriguez
Footfree and Fancyloose by Elizabeth Craft and Sarah Fain

love the one you're with

gossip girl
the carlyles

Created by
Cecily von Ziegesar

Written by
Annabelle Vestry

poppy

LITTLE, BROWN AND COMPANY
New York   Boston

Poppy

Hachette Book Group

237 Park Avenue, New York, NY 10017

For more of your favorite series, visit our website at www.pickapoppy.com

Poppy is an imprint of Little, Brown and Company.

The Poppy name and logo are trademarks of Hachette Book Group, Inc.

First Edition: October 2009

The characters, events, and locations in this book are fictitious. Any similarity to real persons, living or dead, is coincidental and not intended by the author.

alloyentertainment

Produced by Alloy Entertainment

151 West 26th Street, New York, NY 10001

Cover design by Andrea C. Uva

Cover photo by Roger Moenks

ISBN 978-0-316-02067-1

10 9 8 7 6 5 4 3 2 1

CWO

Printed in the United States of America

*It is in vain to say human beings ought to be satisfied
with tranquillity: they must have action;
and they will make it if they cannot find it.*

—Charlotte Brontë, *Jane Eyre*

gossipgirl.net

hey people!

It's November, the time of year when fall drifts to winter and we all start wrapping our cashmere sweaters more tightly around us and thinking about the holidays. In New York, we allow the tourists to enjoy the city, whether they're wobbling around Wollman Rink wearing their blindingly bright puffer jackets or gawking at a larger-than-life SpongeBob SquarePants balloon during the Macy's Thanksgiving Day Parade. It's cold, it's dark, but the windows in Bergdorf's are sparklier than the Marni dresses inside, and all of us Manhattan natives are just itching to celebrate the season in style.

the one thing in our way

Thanksgiving. Who'd have thought a holiday all about gratitude (my short list: sample sales, Corner Bakery coffee, St. Jude's swim team boys running in Central Park without shirts) would have evolved into a four-day calorie-fest all about forced bonding with strange relatives? Luckily, many New Yorkers avoid the awkwardness by heading out of town for the holidays. And who can blame them? Why listen to your drunk uncle drone on about his glory days when you could wear your slinkiest, sexiest Malia Mills string bikini on the beach or your new fur-trimmed boots on the slopes?

So take my advice: Find out who's going AWOL for the holidays, and make sure you get invited along!

A and **J** sharing a dressing room at Barneys, trying on Stella McCartney dresses. They've gone from bitches to besties in the time it takes most people to lose their late-summer tans. . . . **J**, later, at a playground on Bleecker Street, with her on-again boyfriend **J.P.** and two freckly-faced toddlers. Babysitting, or an early visit from the Ghost of Christmas Future? . . . **R**, **O**, and the rest of the swim team guys, drinking pitchers at one of those sticky-floored dives on Second that don't card, ignoring the pack of cougars surrounding them. . . . Lastly, **B** and her best friend, the pierced, tattooed **S**, taking photos in Brooklyn. They're certainly taking *Rancor* seriously!

your e-mail

q:
Dear Gossip Girl,
What's going on for T-Day? You're totally invited to my house. 'Rents are out of town. Suh-weet!
—ponyparty

a:
Dear PP,
While that sounds delightful, I plan to spend my holidays hanging out with people I actually know. But enjoy the free house!
—GG

q:
Dear Gossip Girl,
So, I'm, like, super in love with one of the St. Jude's swim team guys, but they're *always* hanging out together and I feel sort of weird just approaching him in front of all the guys. What should I do?
—swimfan

a: Dear SF,
A hint: Guys are like wildebeests, always traveling in packs for protection and more scared of you than you are of them. They're not nearly so frightening close-up. Try hunting one down on his own and see what happens.
—GG

Just thought of a few more things to add to my list of things to be thankful for: Hot boys, tiny Missoni bikinis, and islands with no drinking age. That's right, I'm joining the legions of New Yorkers getting out of town. Where, you ask? Wouldn't you like to know? But don't pout. You should be thankful that no matter where I am, I'll be keeping track of what anyone who's anyone is doing—on this island *and* any other island worth visiting.

You know you love me,

gossip girl

all in the family

"So, what's up for Thanksgiving? What does your family usually do?" Avery Carlyle asked her friends Jack Laurent and Jiffy Bennett. They were wedged into a cozy leather booth at Amaranth, the café popular with any socialite who needed a cappuccino or a vodka gimlet as a post-Barneys perk-up. It was exactly the type of place Avery had always imagined hanging out in New York.

"Any parties going on?" she continued hopefully, sipping her cappuccino.

In truth, Avery could have done without Thanksgiving. It was just a four-day interruption of her life, which already had everything she could possibly be thankful for.

Well, almost everything.

In September, when she left her childhood home in Nantucket and began her junior year at the ultra-exclusive Constance Billard School for Girls, it seemed like Avery was destined to be one of those unfortunate girls who spend the entire lunch period in the library because they have nowhere else to go. To start with, she and Jack had taken an immediate dislike to each other after fighting over a limited-edition Givenchy satchel at Barneys the day before school began. Tensions quickly escalated until they were outright enemies at Constance Billard, and Avery was completely ostracized by her classmates. Then when Avery scored a coveted internship at *Metropolitan* magazine and was asked to rat out Jack's secrets to a pushy gossip reporter, she'd proved to herself and her Upper East Side peers that she was better than that. She'd finally won them over.

Now she and Jack were friends, and for the past month Avery had *finally* been living the New York City life she'd imagined, full of cocktail parties, gallery openings, and café dates like the one they were having now.

"God, I don't even want to think about Thanksgiving. I have to go with my parents to Beatrice and Deptford's house in Greenwich. If Deptford doesn't die first, that is." Jiffy shrugged as she shoved a slice of avocado in her mouth. She was a petite pug-nosed girl with long bangs that fell over her brown eyes, and five stubborn pounds that kept her from fitting into her older sister Beatrice's discarded couture. Beatrice was thirty-two, a constant fixture on the society circuit, and had her own column in *Page Six* magazine, where she overshared details about her marriage to her seventy-five-year-old fiancé.

As if we really want to know.

"I'll be in hell with the stepbrats." Jack stabbed her napoleon pastry with a fork. The chocolate crumbled on the delicate white plate in a cloud of cocoa powder.

"It can't be that bad, right? I mean, at least they have a nanny," Avery offered, eyeing her friend. Jack was always beautiful, but lately, she'd had shadows under her eyes that even La Mer under-eye cream couldn't hide.

Jack's life was sort of like an H&M dress: From far away, it looked really fashionable and put together. Not only did Jack actually make bitchiness and vanity seem like character attributes, but she was practically a professional ballerina and was dating J. P. Cashman, the son of one of the wealthiest real-estate moguls in the world and a genuinely nice guy. But up close, Jack's life was basically coming apart at the seams, particularly her home life. Her mom was a French former ballerina who was currently filming a reality show in Paris, and Jack was now living with—and serving as an unpaid babysitter to—her dad, stepmom, and two stepsisters in her dad's West Village town house.

"Hey gorgeous!"

Avery looked up, even though she automatically knew it was J.P., there to pick up Jack. He was the only guy Avery knew who could use the word *gorgeous* and not sound totally lame or totally gay.

An important quality in a boyfriend.

J.P. plopped down on the empty chair next to Jack. He had brown hair and brown eyes, and was wearing a black wool overcoat and black dress pants. He looked like a young stockbroker rather than a Riverside Prep junior. "So, what are you guys up to?" he asked conversationally, his fingers playing in Jack's auburn hair.

"J.P.!" Jack's tone was playful, but she batted his hand away and carefully hooked her auburn hair behind her ears.

"Discussing Thanksgiving plans." Avery smiled shyly. Even though she was happy J.P. and Jack were back together, she always felt a pang of loneliness when she saw such a cute couple. Why couldn't *she* find someone who loved her like that?

"We were actually just heading out," Jack said, already scraping back her chair. She rifled through her mist gray leather Chloé wallet and tossed her AmEx on the table. Instantly, a white-shirted waiter picked it up.

"Sure." Avery glanced at her reflection in the gold mirror above the bar and pulled a black-and-white checkered wool Marc Jacobs hat over the tips of her ears. Even though it was only November, the temperature had been freezing, and the weather reports had been forecasting snow all week.

The four of them tumbled outside into the cold twilight.

"Brrr!" Jiffy shivered and pulled her green felt Marc by Marc Jacobs coat closer around her shoulders. "Do you guys want to come to my place?" she asked hopefully.

"We've got to go. We're grabbing a cab downtown." Jack grabbed J.P.'s elbow and held up her leather-gloved hand. "See you guys!" she called as a taxi screeched to the curb.

Avery watched as J.P. opened the cab door and Jack eased her willowy body onto the cracked vinyl seat. It was like a carefully choreographed dance they'd done many times before.

Unlike some things, which they haven't done at all.

"So, what are you doing for Turkey Day?" Jiffy asked Avery as they turned up the street.

"I don't know. I guess it'll just be our family." Avery wasn't really certain. Ever since her mom had gotten serious with her new boyfriend, the triplets weren't sure what the holidays would be like, and so far no one had had the guts to ask. Plus, Avery had been having too much fun getting to know the real New York to nose into her mother's plans. For the past month, she'd been spending every minute not at school with Jack, Jiffy, Genevieve, and Sarah Jane. She loved everything about it: finding the cool restaurants, the parties, the bars and clubs that didn't card. But recently, she'd had an antsy feeling that *something* was about to change.

By *something* does she mean a boyfriend?

"Are any of your brother's friends single?" Jiffy asked, as if reading her mind.

"A couple," Avery replied.

They walked companionably uptown, past the plate-glass windows of the Madison Avenue stores, all of which were already decorated in festive reds, silvers, and greens. Jiffy hurried to catch up to Avery's long stride, switching her two shiny black Barneys bags from one arm to the other. "Do you like any of them?"

"Not really," Avery said evasively. She didn't want to tell Jiffy that she actually had a teeny-tiny crush on her brother's best friend, Rhys. It wasn't that she didn't trust Jiffy. It was more that she was worried if she actually admitted that she liked Rhys, nothing would happen.

Avery was a romantic at heart, and lately she was beginning to think it was something of a curse. Back when she was thirteen, she used to write actual messages in bottles and throw them into the ocean, certain that *some* European royalty would find her message, washed up on some faraway shore on the other side of the Atlantic. Obviously, she wasn't writing messages in bottles anymore, but for some reason, she couldn't figure out how to find guys. Sure, there were tons of guys around, but she went to an all-girl school, and it wasn't like she could just *advertise* that she was looking for a boyfriend.

Is the Internet the modern way to send a message in a bottle?

"Well, we can't all be like Jack and J.P." Jiffy shrugged. "You know, Beatrice knows some good guys."

Avery cringed, imagining the types of guys Beatrice would try to set her up with. Eighty-year-olds? Ninety-year-olds? No thank you. She might be desperate, but she wasn't *that* desperate.

Yet.

"Maybe," Avery said noncommittally. They were already on Seventy-second Street. "Have a great Thanksgiving! Call me if you get bored." She air-kissed Jiffy on both cheeks, then hurriedly walked west toward Fifth, her head bowed against the cold and her shoulders hunched in her bright blue Theory peacoat. She pushed through the revolving door of her building, enjoying the blast of hot air that greeted her in the lobby.

"Miss Carlyle." Jim, her favorite doorman, offered a grandfatherly smile.

"Hi," Avery said as her patent leather Miu Miu Mary Janes clicked on the polished surface of the floors. The sprawling yet tasteful green-marble-and-gold lobby was already decorated for the holidays, with a small tree in the corner and garlands of holly winding around the doorman's desk. She *really* didn't want to spend her first Christmas season in New York alone. Maybe Jiffy was right and she did need a boyfriend plan.

Perhaps the doorman has a son . . .

"Hold the elevator!" a male voice boomed from several feet away. Avery stuck her hand between the doors.

"Avery!"

"Hi!" Avery squeaked, looking up at Remington Wallis, her mom's six-foot-two boyfriend. His face was ruddy from the cold and his arms were laden with vegetable-filled plastic bags. His salt-and-pepper hair was almost George Clooney–ish and he wore Patagonia khakis, a pink button-down shirt, and a black Gore-Tex vest. He looked like he'd just returned from Aspen, though judging from his haul of groceries, he'd been at the Union Square greenmarket. No one would ever imagine that his net worth was in the billions and that he was a regular on *Fortune*'s list of wealthiest people. He just looked like a goofy suburban dad.

"The bag is ripping. Can you do me a favor and hold this?" Remington asked as he plucked an oblong butternut squash from the bag and held it toward Avery. "Your mother loves squash."

Avery smiled fondly. For other Upper East Siders, that sentence would have referred to the game, not a root vegetable. But Edie was different, always preferring homemade batiked dresses to a closet of couture.

Remington and Edie had known each other growing up in New York City. They'd dated in high school, but after graduation, Edie had headed to San Francisco to follow the Grateful Dead and had soon gotten pregnant with the triplets after a freewheeling summer of selling hemp jewelry with some hippie friends. Remington, on the other hand, had followed in the footsteps of his Wallis forefathers: Yale for undergrad and Harvard for business school. He'd set up a hedge fund and became a Wall Street wunderkind, married a socialite, then divorced her once her notorious cheating blew up in scandal. After that he retired, spending time with his daughter and using his money to fund art projects—the more eccentric, the better. He and Edie met again when Remington underwrote a Brooklyn exhibit that featured one of Edie's abstract installations of oversize chinchilla-shaped sculptures.

"Of course." Avery smiled as she awkwardly attempted to balance the squash against her cranberry-colored pebbled-leather Marc Jacobs bag. Even though she was still getting used to her mom *dating*—which Edie had never done when the triplets were growing up—she could see that Remington really cared for her.

The elevator slowly made its way up to the fourteenth floor.

The door slid open and Remington gestured for Avery to step out first.

"Hello, darlings!" Edie opened the door to the Carlyles' penthouse apartment as if on cue. Her earrings, made from tiny silver salt spoons, jangled loudly. She wore a belted white dress that looked like a bathrobe and a pair of red clogs that no one, not even Norwegian folk dancers, should ever wear. But because she was still a rail-thin size two and had large blue eyes and blond hair with only a few streaks of gray, even Avery had to admit her mom could kind of get away with ridiculous fashion choices.

"Oh, Remington." Edie shook her head fondly when she caught sight of the squash, still cradled in Avery's arms like an oddly shaped newborn. "You always know how to surprise me!" Edie tenderly took the squash from Avery and threw her arms around Remington.

Avery politely looked away, concentrating on the abstract red-and-white painting that had appeared in the foyer overnight. Avery squinted. Was that a Picasso? It was either the real thing, or something Remington had discovered by some no-name artist in Brooklyn.

She trailed a safe distance after her mother and Remington down the winding, polished floor of their cavernous penthouse and into the kitchen.

"Hey!" her sister, Baby, called. Baby's wavy, unbrushed brown hair was pulled into a loose ponytail and she was hunched over the marble countertop of the island in the center of the kitchen, looking through pictures on her digital camera. Their brother, Owen, was rummaging through the refrigerator, his white-blond hair still damp from swim practice, wearing his threadbare gray

Nantucket Pirates T-shirt. He was probably looking for a can of Red Bull. He drank at least three a day.

"Hey Ave!" Owen called cheerfully, holding up the silver and blue can in mock salute.

"Remington and I are going to make dinner!" Edie announced grandly. She flung open the walnut cabinets flanking the far wall and began pulling out brightly colored Le Creuset casserole dishes. "Some sort of harvest medley. I'll figure it out."

Avery sighed inwardly. Sometimes her mother's off-the-cuff recipes tasted delicious, but more often than not, she treated cooking as just another artistic experiment.

"How about you let me handle it?" Remington asked. "I could do squash ravioli with sage," he mused, pulling a variety of spices off the spice rack and furrowing his salt-and-pepper brows. He turned to the triplets. "It's a special occasion—my daughter Layla is in town from Oberlin and is coming over for dinner," he explained.

"We're so excited for you all to meet her," Edie said. She gazed at her children as if imagining her brood expanding. "And yes, why don't you do the cooking, darling. Remington went to culinary school," Edie explained proudly, resting her chin on Remington's shoulder as she peered over the counter.

"Just a year or two ago. Once I stopped working full-time and Layla went to college, I decided to just spend some time exploring my passions. That's also about the time I got involved with the Brooklyn Art Collective. But of course, now I have my one favorite passion!" Remington wrapped his beefy arms around Edie's slim waist and gave her a long kiss on the lips.

Okay, we get the point.

Avery sat down at the kitchen island next to Baby. "Do you know what we're doing for Thanksgiving?" She lowered her voice as she glanced from Baby's deep coffee-colored eyes to Owen's bright blue ones.

"I don't know." Owen shook his head. "Is *he* part of our plans?" he asked, an edge to his voice as he glanced sideways at Remington and Edie.

"No idea. But you can bet it'll probably be the usual mix of randoms," Baby said with an affectionate eye-roll. Back in Nantucket, Edie would always invite stray people who didn't have anywhere else to go for the holidays. Last year, the dinner party guests had included a stern sea captain from Sweden named Oleg, a 93-year-old Boston society hostess who'd been uninvited to her own Thanksgiving after telling her entire extended family she was giving her estate to the Feral Cat Society, and a couple in their thirties who drove from state to state, occasionally setting up lawn chairs next to a sign that said TALK TO US!

"What are we talking about?" Edie floated past on her way to the Sub-Zero to put away the greenmarket produce she wasn't going to cook.

"What are we doing for Thanksgiving?" Avery asked innocently. "Because if we're not doing anything special, I think I might go keep Jack company. She's going through a rough time with her family," Avery explained.

"I could come if Jack needs strength in numbers," Owen offered, grabbing a brownie from a plate on the counter and stuffing it in his mouth.

"Remington actually has a little announcement to make. Remington?" Edie called to the other end of the kitchen, where Remington was manning the six-burner stove.

"Ah, yes!" He wiped his hands on the back of his pants and walked over to the counter.

"As you know, your mom is very important to me. And you kids have all become important to me." Remington awkwardly leaned over to try to ruffle Owen's blond hair. Owen, who at six foot two was not exactly hair-ruffling height, ducked away. "So, I thought we could all go away together. You three, Edie and I, and Layla—it'll be a great way for us to all get to know each other. I've booked us a few villas on Shelter Cay. I used to own the island. I sold the property years ago, but it's still one of my favorite places." Remington drifted back to the stove, as if he'd just announced they were going out to dinner.

"Your island?" Avery asked in confusion.

"Just a small one in the Bahamas. It was one of my first investments. But they still treat me well there." Remington smiled.

"Isn't that terrific?" Edie said, her eyes shining. "Of course, if you kids have anyone you want to bring—like maybe your friend Jack?—you're welcome to. The more the merrier! Everyone should have *fun* on Thanksgiving," Edie said definitively.

"Sure, thanks!" Avery said, excited. A tropical vacation and she could bring Jack? She pushed the plate of brownies away as if it was contaminated. She had so much to do! She needed a new bathing suit, and a few new Lilly Pulitzer dresses, and a self-tanner appointment at Bliss. . . . She quickly pulled her pink Filofax out of her bag.

"Great," Owen muttered, practically stomping out of the kitchen.

"Wait!" Avery commanded, hurrying after him.

"Owen," Baby said, sliding off her chair and following her brother and sister down the hallway like the loyal sibling she was.

"I can't believe this!" Owen exclaimed once they were in his bedroom. Back when they were little, they used to have triplet meetings in their backyard tree house. They hadn't had one in ages. Now, standing on Owen's dirty laundry–covered floor, Avery felt both old and young. "He's been dating mom for, like, a *month*," Owen spat angrily.

"Calm down. They're in love. You don't need to be an asshole just because this year there won't be any tofurkey to cook. Is that why you're upset?" Baby teased. Ever since Owen was twelve, he'd taken it upon himself to be in charge of Thanksgiving dinner.

"No." Clearly, Owen was not in the mood. "It's just . . . who is this guy, telling us what we're doing for Thanksgiving?" He plopped down on his flannel-sheeted bed and looked at his sisters, who both had their arms crossed and were staring down at him like mismatched bookends.

"So, let me get this straight. Would you prefer if Mom invited her Brooklyn artist friends and had us all spend the day doing performance art?" Baby asked.

"We probably won't even see them once we get there, right?" Avery pointed out. "Anyway, it's nice that they want us to invite friends. You should bring Rhys," she suggested, changing the subject.

In the most subtle of ways.

"I guess so. Look, I think I'm going to skip the 'family' dinner and head over to Hugh's. He's having some people over." Owen went into the bathroom and closed the door. The triplet meeting was clearly over.

"Fine!" Baby said in a singsongy voice, not wanting to indulge Owen's pouty mood.

"Fine," Avery echoed. Owen was being seriously immature, but if he was going to hang out with the swim team guys, he'd have the perfect opportunity to invite Rhys on vacation. Avery could picture herself on a beach, in her Milly bikini, the salty air blowing through her hair as a bare-chested Rhys offered her a daiquiri with a dainty straw. "Fine," she said again, but it was better than fine. It was *perfect*.

Here's hoping Mr. Manners doesn't have plans of his own.

b meets her match

Remington looked up from the green beans he was sautéing. "Baby, I hope you don't mind, but I took a look at some of your photographs."

Baby glanced up from her cell, where she'd just texted Sydney with an invite to the Bahamas. Next to Remington was the digital camera Baby had left on the table, filled with shots she had taken this weekend, for *Rancor*, the school's art magazine. It was run by her best friend, Sydney Miller, a multi-pierced and tattooed girl who described her sexuality as "flexual." Baby had always been sort of interested in photography, but had only been taking pictures with an artistic sensibility for the past couple of months.

"I like to look at art while I'm cooking. It inspires me," Remington added. Weird banjo music filled the room, and he was shuffling from one earth-friendly woven hemp moccasin to the other.

"Oh," Baby replied uncertainly as she retrieved the camera.

"I couldn't help myself. You've got an amazing sense of perspective. Just like your mom," Remington said thoughtfully, as he passed Baby a clove of garlic. "Mind chopping that?"

"Sure." Baby took a knife and began slicing the white clove into teeny-tiny squares. Even though she'd just made a mental note to hide everything in the apartment from now on, Remington was nice, and actually pretty cool, as old men went. And Baby was just happy her mom was happy.

"You know, Baby, my daughter, Layla, is just a few years older than you. She's a sophomore at Oberlin. Smarter than me, that's for sure. A straight-A philosophy and math double major. I think you and she will really get along," Remington mused proudly. He peered over her shoulder. "Good chopping!"

Baby smiled, pleased with the compliment. Just then, her cell beeped with a reply from Sydney.

You elitist bitch! Sorry but I have to spend Thanksgiving in Bedford with the senile grandma, so she can be disappointed in me before she dies. Thinking of what else I can pierce/tattoo before then. Have fun for me. I won't.

Baby smiled at her friend's allover randomness. Knowing Sydney, she probably *would* get a tattoo before Thanksgiving. She already had a star on her arm and a fish on her ankle.

Maybe she could consolidate and get a starfish on her ass.

"Your friend coming?" Remington asked, not even turning around. It was weird how he seemed to notice *everything.*

"No," Baby mumbled, her excitement dwindling. Without Sydney, she was staring down a string of days hanging out alone. After all, Avery would be with Jack, trying on sundresses and drinking mojitos and whatever the hell else their newfound best friendship was based on, while Owen and Rhys would swim and run and parasail together. *But,* Baby thought, *it's the beach!* Even if she just sat on the sand alone with a book, she'd be happy.

The doorbell rang, interrupting Baby's thoughts. "I'll get it," she announced. Remington smiled gratefully, his hands covered with the gooey orange innards of the squash.

Baby ran to the front entranceway, swung open the door, and found herself face-to-face with a petite girl with crazy blond curls piled under an enormous purple wool knit hat. She wore an oversize gray American Apparel dress, black leggings, and a huge, furry brown sweater instead of a coat. She was carrying a large black guitar case covered with stickers from old-school girl bands like Bikini Kill and Sleater-Kinney and Le Tigre. She looked cool and like she didn't give a fuck.

"Hello?" Baby asked suspiciously. Was this really Remington's daughter? She didn't look like a math-and-whatever double major at all. In fact, she looked a little bit like a girlier version of Sydney.

Ask and you shall receive. . . .

"You must be Baby. Or are you Avery?" the girl asked in a lilting voice. She dropped her duffel on the floor, then pulled off her hat and shook her blondish-brown hair out of her face. "I know it's so weird, but I feel like we need to hug. I'm Layla Wallis," she said as she pulled Baby into an embrace. Layla smelled sort of like patchouli, and they were exactly the same height of five foot zero.

"Yeah, I'm Baby. Nice to meet you. My sister's . . . somewhere." Baby shrugged. She pointed curiously to the guitar. "You play?"

"Yeah, my boyfriend and I are in a band together. Do you?" Layla asked, an eager grin spreading across her face. Baby shook her head. Maybe she could learn, though. She wondered idly if Layla might be able to teach her.

"Layla!" Remington strode across the room, easily picking up his daughter and swinging her around.

"Is she here?" Edie's voice carried from her studio. "Layla, darling, you're more stunning in person than in pictures!" Edie cooed as she walked into the foyer. There was a smudge of green paint on her high forehead.

"So, how's the math going?" Remington asked jovially, setting Layla down.

"Daaad," Layla rolled her eyes, mock annoyed. "You *know* I'm not majoring in math. I changed to gender studies. Women's studies was too limiting," she explained to Baby. "Besides, I figured, why not get as useless a degree as possible to annoy my father?" Layla shrugged and looked over at Baby, as if they were sharing an inside joke. Baby smiled back, just glad to be included. Owen and Avery were still in their rooms, probably calling Rhys and Jack and planning their fun buddy-trip at this very second. But suddenly it seemed like Baby might have a buddy of her own.

"Anyway, Edie, thank you so much for having me. My father told me you were an artist; I'd love to see your work," Layla said sincerely. Edie positively beamed.

"So, tell me honestly." Layla whispered conspiratorially as she and Baby trailed their parents toward the kitchen. "What do you think of my dad?" An impish smile formed on her face.

"He seems cool." Baby shrugged. Really, she was thinking *Layla* seemed cool. Sydney not being able to come no longer seemed like such a big deal.

"Even though he dresses like an eco-yuppie, he's really great. If you could help me with the clothes, it'd be amazing." Layla companionably linked arms with Baby's. "I just know we're going to have so much fun!"

Baby nodded and smiled. She and Layla already had the same

taste in clothes and in music, and they shared a set of crazy-in-love parents. Add to that staying in the same room, and she knew that by the end of this trip, they'd be sharing secrets—they'd be sharing everything.

And she means *everything*.

r gets an assignment

"Fuck!" Owen exclaimed as the doorman opened the door and he stepped out into a downpour. He hadn't bothered to bring an umbrella, and it wasn't like he wanted to go back upstairs to get one. He huddled under the green awning, hoping that a cab would pass by, but Fifth Avenue was practically silent. The chance of getting a cab was about as good as him having a super time during the upcoming family bonding vacation. Hopefully, Rhys would be able to come and they could just hang out as far away as possible—like, preferably another island away—from Remington.

Owen balled his hands in his pockets and began to walk north, toward Hugh Moore's house. Hugh was a teammate from the St. Jude's swim team and had decided to throw an impromptu party when Coach announced they had tomorrow off. Owen had planned on checking out the scene at Hugh's after dinner, but once Remington announced his plan, he'd lost his appetite. It wasn't like Remington was a bad guy. If he were the dad of one of his buddies, he'd be pretty cool. But everything just seemed a little *sudden*. After years of never dating, his mom was practically married to this guy.

He reached Hugh's town house on Eightieth and Park. The limestone steps were flanked by two large lion sculptures. Owen patted one on the head as he jogged up the steps, and rang the bell.

"Hello, sir!" Hugh flung open both of the large black oak double doors. He wore a velvet jacket belted loosely around his frame, possibly in an attempt to look like Hugh Hefner. Hugh sometimes bragged that the *Playboy* founder was his namesake.

"Fuck, you're wet," Hugh noted, shaking his head. Hugh was a muscle-y blond junior whose home was the de facto St. Jude's swim team party house, since his parents were practically always traveling in Europe. He ushered Owen down a large mirror-paneled hallway. "I'm trying to change up this gathering a little. Maybe give some of our guys something to do this weekend. Just follow my lead."

"Sounds good, man." Owen was glad to have something to think about besides his mom's love life. "What's the master plan this time?"

"Basically, our pansy teammates aren't getting action. And it's like, sometimes you have to bring the fucking mountain to them," Hugh said cryptically as he flung open the glass-framed French doors to a large formal living room. Kids were lounging in the leather wingback chairs and stiff leather couches, Riedel highball glasses in hand. A projector screen flashed some weird movie against the wall, the images distorting the large Manet painting hanging over the fireplace.

"Look who's here!" Hugh called to the motley group. He held out his own glass in a mock toast. Owen glanced around. Amongst the usual crew of varsity and JV swimmers were a couple of random girls he'd never seen before. "Ladies, for those of you who don't know, this is Owen Carlyle. Owen, this is Sabine, Salome, Sabrina, and Simone. These lovely ladies agreed to come to our French film-fest. They're all in Le Cinéma Français Society at L'École. It's sort of like a cultural exchange program, with alcohol and nudity." Hugh leered up at the wall. The image was grainy, but the characters on-screen were definitely naked.

"Right now, we're watching Bertolucci. *Last Tango in Paris*. A masterpiece," he explained to Owen.

Owen nodded. So that was Hugh's plan: to act like an artsy, sensitive, foreign film–loving guy when he really just wanted an excuse to screen a pseudo-porn movie in mixed company. And with girls from L'École, nonetheless—the girls from the all-female French school had a reputation for being, ahem, looser than their American counterparts. They certainly seemed to develop faster.

"Hey." Owen flashed a smile at the four girls. Each of them smiled back.

Parlez-vous français?

"Here's a seat," said one, practically shoving puppyish freshman Chadwick Jenkins off the couch and onto the floor. Chadwick didn't even notice. His eyes were still glued to the screen, where the characters were engaged in some extremely explicit foreplay involving a stick of butter.

"I'm cool, but thanks." Owen scanned the room for Rhys, brushing past another one of the girls Hugh had introduced. She had dyed black hair, a nose ring, and a belly ring Owen could see through her off-white off-the-shoulder T-shirt. What was her name again? It began with an S. . . .

Skanké?

"Hey man!" Rhys called from a corner, standing up hurriedly.

His blue Ralph Lauren polo shirt was unbuttoned, and his dark brown hair was mussed.

"Dude, did you see that girl I was sitting with? She's crazy," he hissed, pulling Owen into the large, country-modern kitchen. "She's not wearing a bra or underwear. She told me that. Then she showed me. She *showed* me. Is that what girls do now?" Rhys shuddered.

Owen grinned at his uptight buddy. He sounded like his mom, the society hostess of the television show *Tea with Lady Sterling*. It was a talk show about manners in contemporary society, shown in the afternoon and rerun on the screens in the backseats of cabs. For some reason, Avery was obsessed with the show.

"Dude, just grow one," Owen said, not unkindly. "She's not going to bite."

"Oh, she does bite." Rhys rubbed the side of his neck, and Owen could just make out two sets of faint reddish toothmarks. "Seriously, these girls are fucking dangerous," Rhys finished, shaking his head.

"I need a beer," Owen announced. "You need, like, ten," he added, laughing at Rhys's shell-shocked expression.

"You're telling me!" Rhys pulled open the door of one of the two matching Sub-Zero refrigerators that flanked the rear wall of the kitchen. "Happy Thanksgiving," he said, opening the bottle. "First I was attacked by a French vampire girl, and tomorrow I have to wake up at the asscrack of dawn to go to England."

He sat down on one of the stainless steel stools surrounding the marble island in the center of the kitchen. "Just for once, I'd like to do a real Thanksgiving, you know? Instead I have to go to my awful cousins' awful manor house. You know what we do there? Go on a foxhunt. It sucks." Rhys shook his head grimly.

"Well, consider this your lucky year." Owen chugged his own beer, slamming the empty bottle against the hammered stainless steel counter. "We're all going to the Bahamas. It's this lame family bonding trip with my mom's boyfriend," Owen explained. He couldn't say the word *boyfriend* without cringing. It wasn't like he wanted his mom to be lonely or alone, but she and Remington had only been dating for a little over a month. Still, there was the prospect of warm weather, lots of booze, foreign girls . . . "Anyway, you're invited."

"Seriously? They'd be cool with that?" Rhys's eyes lit up.

"Of course they would. You should come. It'd be good for you to get away," Owen said. Rhys had seemed a little down ever since his breakup with Kelsey at the beginning of the year. Owen generally tried to avoid the subject, since he had pretty much single-handedly destroyed that relationship when he and Kelsey hooked up. But now he and Rhys were both over Kelsey. What better way to *really* smooth things over than a bachelor weekend?

"What's going on, men?" Hugh appeared in the kitchen, a drunken Sabine clinging to him for support. She was the same one who'd bitten Rhys. The strap of her tank top had fallen off her shoulder, her skirt barely covered her super-skinny ass, and she looked way too drunk for 7 p.m.

"I was looking for you guys," Hugh continued. "Sabine and I decided it'd be educational for us all to do some reenactments. You know, to fully understand the context of the film."

"I can show you what you missed," Sabine said, pulling the other strap of her tank top off her shoulder, as if she were ready to strip right in the middle of Hugh's kitchen. "What do you think, Rhys?" Rhys wordlessly shook his head and shot a pleading look at Owen to rescue him.

"We were just coming out," Owen said, blushing as soon as the words left his mouth. Earlier in the school year, when he was hooking up with Kelsey covertly, the guys on the team had thought he was being secretive because he was gay. Even now, when it was common knowledge he'd basically stolen Kelsey from Rhys, he was still sensitive about gay jokes.

"You know I'm nothing but supportive." Hugh waggled his eyebrows. "Do whatever you want, guys!"

"What are they going to do?" Sabine slurred, obviously angry that no one seemed to notice her impromptu striptease.

"Carlyle and I are going to the Bahamas," Rhys explained.

Because *that* doesn't sound gay.

"Oh! You need a goodbye kiss!" Sabine pulled up her tank top straps as she lurched toward Rhys. She dragged her red-painted fingernails against the back of his neck as she pulled him toward her. Rhys took an automatic step backward. What the hell? Since when were girls so *predatory*? Sure, she was hot, but she was also hammered. He didn't want just a drunken hookup. Whatever happened to romance?

Don't ask the girl who thinks tequila shots are foreplay.

"I . . . uh, have to pack," Rhys said desperately.

"No you don't." Sabine made puppy-dog eyes at him. "You know what I always say?" She leaned closer to Rhys so he could smell the tequila and Life Savers on her breath. "*Je ne regrette rien.*"

Suddenly, a look of terror flashed across her face. "I don't feel so good!" she apologized, throwing open one of the doors to the terrace. Rhys could hear retching sounds.

"Happens to the best of us," Hugh called out cheerfully. He turned back to the guys, his face now serious. "Listen, Rhys. You have to do more than pack," he announced, thoughtfully stroking his bearded chin. At the beginning of the school year, as a show of solidarity after Kelsey broke up with Rhys, the swim team had made a pact that all of them would stop shaving, and that none of them would get action until Rhys had. The rest of the team had abandoned the plan after a few weeks, but Hugh had soldiered on. The fact that facial hair made it easier for him to avoid getting carded was certainly a plus. "You need to lose your virginity, stat. And here's your opportunity. Sometimes it's easier to get outside of your comfort zone if you're in a different geographic region. It expands your thought horizons and stuff like that. You better get laid in the Bahamas. If you don't, I don't even want to see you back here," Hugh finished, as if that settled the matter. "I'll go make sure she's okay," he added, and went outside to check on Sabine.

Rhys shook his head at Hugh's lewd suggestion. It was true—he was still a virgin. The swim team guys had been trying to get him to lose his V card this entire year. It wasn't like he hadn't had any opportunities: At any given party, he could pull a girl like Sabine away to one of the guest rooms upstairs and just get it over with. But he didn't *want* that. He wanted a nice girl whom he could go to dinner with, kiss while watching romantic comedies, make playlists for and send cute e-mails to. And then, when they were ready, they could have sex. And have it actually *mean* something.

This week on *Tea with Lady Sterling*: freak-of-nature high school boys.

"You okay?" Owen asked Rhys sympathetically, once they were alone again. He pulled out two more beers and placed them on the counter. He knew Rhys had been bent out of shape over the whole virginity thing. He'd wanted to lose it to Kelsey, only to discover Kelsey had lost *hers* to Owen. It was pretty messed up, actually, and Owen really hoped Rhys would be able to put the past behind him and move on.

"Better than *her*." Rhys gestured toward Sabine's still-retching form. Okay, so he sort of felt like a loser.

"You better not come back from the Bahamas a virgin," Hugh called from the terrace, where he was rubbing Sabine's back. "Carlyle, make sure of it!" he added.

Thus spoke the Master of Multitasking.

Rhys considered this. As drunk as Hugh was, he had a point. Why *not* just lose it in the Bahamas? Maybe out of New York, and out of his mom's sight, he'd be able to lose his hang-ups. Maybe if he just got it over with, away from Hugh and the swim team guys, he'd be in a better place to find a *real* relationship once he got back. He needed to stop acting like a shy pansy.

"I'm going to do it!" Rhys announced. He drained the entire Sierra Nevada in one gulp and slammed down the empty bottle as if in victory. "Watch me!"

Not literally, we hope. . . .

home for the holidays

"Do you want to watch *Belle de Jour* or *Amélie*?" Jack called to J.P. as she rifled through the DVDs in her dad's lame collection. Even though Jack had been living in her dad's Bank Street town house for over a month, she didn't think of it as her home. She definitely didn't feel like she belonged there.

The rest of the world—including the Laurents' Irish nanny, Saoirse—had begun their Thanksgiving holiday tonight. But Jack had to stay home with Colette and Elodie, her three-year-old twin stepsisters. Luckily J.P. had come over to help out. Jack wrinkled her nose as she yanked open the glass cabinet next to the flat-screen television and flipped past an entire collection of Gérard Depardieu films. Her dad had such an embarrassingly obvious French fetish.

"I don't care," J.P. called from the adjacent playroom.

"What are you doing?" Jack stood and pulled her jeans further up her hips. Her Antik Denims had felt a tiny bit tight when she put them on this morning, and they definitely weren't the best pants for crawling around on the floor.

She stood in the doorway of the pink-and-purple playroom,

where J.P. was wedged into a chair at a tiny white wooden table, a pink teacup balanced on his knee. Elodie sat across from him, and Colette was in the corner of the room, lying on Theo, a stuffed polar bear that had been Jack's when she was a child. Originally white, now the oversize stuffed animal was a dingy gray. Jack had never liked stuffed animals, but it still bothered her that her dad had gone through all of the trouble to *save* the toy, only to give it to the stepbrats.

"Tea?" J.P. asked. He winked as he held the cup out to her.

"Jack's not invited!" Colette cried, jumping off Theo as if to physically bar Jack from entering the room.

"No, she's not. J.P. is ours!" Elodie added.

"Well, good, because I don't like tea. I only like vodka." Jack tried to sound less annoyed than she felt. Who were *they* to tell her she wasn't invited to their tea party? She was their sister, for fuck's sake!

"I think we could arrange a private v-o-d-k-a party," J.P. said, raising an eyebrow.

"Guess what, girls? It's bedtime!" Jack lied. Her Rolex only said seven thirty. Not like they knew how to tell time, thank God.

It was strange to actually spend time with the stepbrats, after years of pretending they didn't exist. Colette and Elodie both had light blond hair like their former yoga instructor mom, Rebecca, but their freckly faces and slightly upturned noses looked like Jack's when she was a toddler. Of course, even back when Jack was three, she wouldn't have been caught dead in the Pepto-Bismol pink matching Bonpoint outfits Rebecca had dressed them in.

"No!" Elodie whined.

"Vodka!" Colette yelled randomly as she wandered over to J.P., wrapping her arms around him. Elodie crossed her arms and stuck her tongue out at Jack.

"Sorry, girls. Party's over. It's bedtime for me, too." J.P. stood up awkwardly, Colette still clinging to his khaki-clad leg.

"You okay, gorgeous?" J.P. whispered into Jack's auburn hair.

Jack nodded, even though she felt kind of weird. She knew it should be adorable to watch her boyfriend play with her step-siblings, but it wasn't. Watching J.P. with Colette and Elodie was like watching her life, fast-forwarded ten years. Was this what it was going to be like when they had kids?

"Come *on*!" Jack leaned down and pried Colette's disconcertingly sticky hand off J.P.'s leg.

"Ow!" Colette whined. "You *hurted* me. Mean Jack!"

"Mean Jack!" Elodie chanted, using her tiny hands to hit Jack's knees.

"Bed," Jack hissed, hooking her hands under Elodie's armpits and picking her up. "If you don't go to bed, you might never see Theo again."

Colette's large blue eyes widened in horror. She opened her tiny mouth and let out a wail. Elodie soon followed suit. *Fan-fucking-tastic.*

"Okay, ladies!" J.P. leaned down and scooped up Colette, then deftly grabbed Elodie from Jack. He balanced one twin on each hip as if he'd been doing this for years. "Jack was just kidding about Theo. Ready for bed?"

"*No!*" Elodie shouted. Colette took up the chorus, their fair, freckly faces turning a dangerous, tomato red.

"Want to just put in a movie they can watch until they fall asleep? It might be easier," J.P. suggested quietly.

"Fine." Jack sighed as she stalked back to the overstuffed Jonathan Adler leather club chair.

"We *love* J.P.!" Colette yelled.

"This is okay, right?" J.P. asked Jack, already rifling through the shelves of developmentally appropriate DVDs.

"Movie!" Elodie yelled, stomping her tiny foot.

"Okay, movie!" J.P. said. "Do you like this one?" He held up a *Dora the Explorer* DVD case.

"Yes, yes, yes!" the girls yelled in chorus. J.P. stuck the disc into the DVD player and the twins immediately fell silent, entranced by the show.

Jack pulled her phone out of her jeans pocket. She wasn't sure who to call. Sarah Jane had been in Aspen since Monday, Jiffy and Genevieve were crashing a lame benefit party that Beatrice was hosting, and Avery had a family dinner. Still, she needed to do *something* to distract her from her ridiculous night.

She was *supposed* to be drinking a large well-deserved glass of Côtes du Rhône, eating cheese and crackers, and contemplating the fact that in just two days, she and J.P. were going to do it. *It* it. They'd been so close for so long, but finally, they had special Thanksgiving plans—a cozy, private rendezvous. Jack's dad, Rebecca, and the stepbrats were all planning to go to New Jersey to celebrate with Rebecca's extended family, so she'd have the entire town house to herself for the night. All J.P. had to do was come over after he'd had dinner with his family. It would be perfect. After all, one month after their *what were we thinking?* breakup where J.P. had spent less than a week dating Baby Carlyle, they were stronger than ever.

Jack felt stronger than ever too. Sure, living with her dad, Rebecca, and the stepbrats wasn't ideal, but normally the toddlers had their nanny to amuse them. Jack's ballet classes had never been better, and her teachers were talking to her about conservatory programs for college. Even her friendships were good. While she'd have preferred it if Avery weren't related to Baby, Avery had turned out to be more interesting than she'd originally thought. She had a snarky side to her, and would definitely let Jack know if her butt looked flat in her jeans. She'd never really met anyone like that before.

As if on cue, her phone burst into *The Nutcracker Suite.* Avery.

"I'll go upstairs," Jack announced. Not like it mattered. J.P. was laughing along with the twins at Dora, looking like he was having the fucking time of his life.

"What's up?" Jack asked as she stepped into the upstairs den. Rebecca had an unfortunate Danish modern-and-pastel fetish. Jack settled into the ugly low salmon-colored couch.

"Sorry, I know you're with J.P.! I hope I'm not interrupting anything," Avery's voice was teasing on the other end.

"Nope, it's preschool power hour here." Jack sighed. "Seriously, remind me to never have kids. I can't even talk about it." She shuddered. "How's your family?" she asked. Even though they were getting close, she didn't want Avery to know just how pathetic her life was.

"Good, actually—I just found out we're going to the Bahamas tomorrow!" Avery squealed. "My mom's boyfriend invited us. Can you come? I think Owen's bringing Rhys. It'll be *soooo* much fun! Please?"

Jack sighed heavily. Part of her really wanted to go. She knew she and Avery would have a blast together, and it felt like forever since she'd gotten out of the city. But she didn't want to postpone *it* again. The four-day weekend was the perfect time. Tomorrow, she'd go shopping for new lingerie; Thursday, she'd officially become a woman; and then Friday, Saturday, and Sunday she and J.P. would repeat the performance. After all, your first time was supposed to be sort of clumsy, so Jack wanted to have at least one good experience before school on Monday, where she'd dangle not-telling details in front of her friends and watch their faces go green with envy.

Practice *does* make perfect.

"I understand if you can't," Avery said, recognizing Jack's silence as a no. "I know it's hard to leave J.P. and stuff."

"Yeah, I have to stay. I'm sorry." Jack sighed. She *did* feel sorry—a little sorry for herself, actually. If she and J.P. had already had sex, like normal people, she could go on vacation with Avery and have fun and not worry about planning out every second of her four-day holiday like some desperate housewife.

"No, I totally understand," Avery said sweetly. She sounded a little disappointed, but happy for Jack. "Have fun!"

"Thanks." Jack sighed, wishing Avery hadn't hung up so quickly. She *really* didn't want to go back down to the playroom. Instead, she gazed out the large bay window. The town house was right next to a coffee shop, and people often sat on the outside steps, sharing a cappuccino or a cigarette. Even though it was cold and rainy, a couple in their twenties were huddled close to each other, their knees hugged to their chests, their foreheads practically touching.

Normally, Jack would want to tell them to fuck off, but right now, she sort of wanted to join them. Anything was better than dealing with the stepbrats. And even though she was excited to spend the long weekend with J.P., part of her wondered if in turning down the trip with Avery, she'd made the right decision. She and Avery always had so much fun together, and they'd be on the beach, soaking in the sun and just taking some time *off*. Of course, Baby Carlyle would be there, and she and Jack weren't exactly the best of friends. But Owen would be there too. Jack felt an involuntary shiver travel down her spine at the thought of him. Earlier this year, Jack and Avery had been in the midst of their turf war, and Baby had just started going out with J.P. Jack, in an effort to make J.P. jealous and to piss Avery off, had basically blackmailed Owen into pretending to be her boyfriend, using the information that he and Kelsey Talmadge—his best friend's girlfriend—had hooked up on the sly. It had totally worked, and now Jack had J.P. back. But spending all that time with Owen, even kissing him for show, Jack had . . . *felt* something. She couldn't explain why, but somehow, even *pretending* to date Owen had felt more real to her than her years of actually dating J.P.

"The monsters fell asleep on the sofa." J.P. appeared in the doorway, snapping Jack back into the present. "I don't want to wake them up," he said, sitting next to Jack in the semi-darkness. She could hear the strains of some counting song emanating from downstairs.

"Good. So, we're alone. . . ." Jack let the sentence trail off. J.P. was sitting very close to her and she could smell his familiar eucalyptus-and-clean-laundry scent. He slid his fingers underneath Jack's pink Tocca cashmere sweater.

"Shh, let's be really quiet," Jack whispered as she slid closer to him. She kissed him urgently, like this was the only thing in the world that mattered. And maybe it was. As J.P.'s fingers trailed down her back, Jack wondered if maybe they should just get it over with, here and now. Who needed all the ceremony? She started to unzip her jeans when there was a loud shriek from the doorway.

"Dora stopped!" Elodie cried, Colette standing just behind her. "We want more Dora!"

J.P. slid away from Jack on the sofa. "I think it's bedtime for you girls," he said gently, moving toward the toddlers and scooping them up easily in each of his arms. "I'll be back in a sec," he said to Jack over his shoulder, but even he didn't sound convinced.

J.P. disappeared upstairs, kids flung over his arms, and Jack felt like a desperate housewife for the second time that night.

for r, it's all about the essentials

"Here's good," Rhys Sterling said on Wednesday morning as his mother's town car almost sailed past Owen's building at Seventy-second and Fifth.

"You want to be let off here?" Oliver, Lady Sterling's driver, glanced at Rhys quizzically in the rearview mirror.

"I know," Rhys muttered. Only his mother would see the need to send him off in a car for a four-block ride. Lady Sterling was all about appearances, and it simply would not have been appropriate for Rhys to walk the four blocks up Fifth Avenue with his Tumi duffel bag slung over his shoulder.

"Well, cheerio!" Oliver the chauffeur said in his British accent as he opened the door for Rhys. "Have a good trip!"

"Thanks!" Rhys grinned. He felt giddy. A week of no family, no responsibilities, and especially no foxhunts sounded fucking *amazing*.

Not to mention the, um, action plan?

"Hey man!"

Rhys whirled around and saw Owen standing outside the building, wearing khakis and a royal blue sweater.

"What are you doing out here?" Rhys asked as he set his bag down on the pavement. Immediately, the doorman picked it up, slung it over his own shoulder, and lugged it inside.

"I had to get out of the apartment," Owen confessed, crossing his arms over his chest. "It's Remington. Dude, I know he and my mom are dating, but they're all over each other. He was feeding her scrambled eggs this morning." Owen shuddered. "In his pj's."

Rhys noticed Owen's strong jaw clenching. That must be hard for him. It was hard enough when he saw his mom and dad get touchy-feely. It always happened after two glasses of sherry.

"Anyway, the doorman will take care of your stuff. I've been dispatched to get supplies. Let's go!" Owen began walking past the stately limestone buildings toward Madison and quickly crossed the street.

"My sister wanted us to stop here," he explained as he stopped in front of the gold doors of Zitomer. Lady Sterling absolutely adored the legendary Upper East Side pharmacy.

"Happy holidays and happy shopping," an older man in a maroon jacket greeted them as they walked in the door.

"I don't really get why Avery doesn't just go to Duane Reade," Owen said, naming the grimy drugstore that was on almost every New York City block. Rhys knew why. It was because Avery loved anything that was *classic*. So did he. When he'd talked to her for the first time last month, on the terrace of the Carlyles', they'd even found out they shared the same taste in old-school Frank Sinatra music.

They worked their way past the cramped aisles of beauty products toward the more traditional drugstore items in the back of the store. A woman with two cats on a leash stood frowning at a candle display, blocking their way.

"Excuse me, can we get through?" Owen blurted. The woman and her cats looked up in annoyance, but let them pass.

"Honestly, Avery owes me after this," Owen called over his shoulder. Rhys blushed involuntarily at Avery's name.

"I'll be right back." Rhys hurriedly shuffled further into the honeysuckle and lemon–scented store, wandering toward the pharmacy area in the back. A display of condoms was discreetly lined up underneath the Formica counter, their bright packages looking almost lewd next to the Emergen-C packets and Carmex surrounding the display. He leaned down and stared at them. He'd thought about the idea of losing his virginity ever since he came home from Hugh's last night. Maybe it wouldn't hurt just to have them on hand. Who knew what the condom situation would be like on a semi-private island?

"Can I help you, young man?" A wiry gray-haired pharmacist wearing a double-breasted white coat leaned over the counter and peered down his thick glasses at Rhys.

"Oh, I . . ." Rhys blushed bright red. The store suddenly felt a million degrees hotter, and he loosened his Burberry scarf. "I've got what I need, thanks." He quickly slid a red-and-black package off the display and hurriedly walked away. He knew there was nothing embarrassing about buying condoms, but it still made him feel sort of pervy.

He spotted Owen's shock of blond hair by the Bliss display in the center of the store.

"Hey man." He squinted at the blue-and-white tube in Owen's hand. *Bliss Oil-Free Sunban Lotion.* "That's really good. It's not greasy," he said thoughtfully. He hated greasy, pore-clogging sunblock and had tried just about every brand before settling on Bliss, or occasionally Clarins.

"Thanks, Your Gayness. It's for *Avery*." Owen rolled his eyes and haphazardly threw a couple tubes in his red plastic shopping basket.

"Oh, she likes it too?" Immediately, Rhys imagined rubbing the lotion into Avery's shoulders. He quickly shook the thought off. She was Owen's *sister*.

"What'd *you* get?" Owen asked, yanking the condoms out of Rhys's hand. "Magnums? Good for you. So, you're really taking Hugh's challenge seriously?"

"Well, I figured it'd be better to be prepared." Rhys shrugged, trying to act nonchalant even though he felt anything but.

"That's true. You know, maybe I'll join you. I mean, not *join* you, but find someone too. I think it'd be good for us to just live it up this week. I mean, why the hell not?" Owen asked rhetorically. He flipped open the sunscreen bottle and took an experimental sniff. "Oh my God, this smells like girl. You really use this, Mr. Magnum?" he teased.

"I like it," Rhys said defensively. "It's better for your skin. You'll be begging to borrow it by the weekend."

"Well, I'm sure *Avery* would love a guy who uses fruity girly products, but—" Owen laughed but then stopped himself. He furrowed his blond brows at Rhys, as if seeing him for the first time. His eyes flicked to the condoms still in Rhys's hand. "Wait, you're not thinking about my *sister*, are you?"

"No!" Rhys said quickly. "Of course not."

Meaning, yes.

"Good." Owen's tone was light, but Rhys knew his message was serious. Owen had always seemed protective of his sisters, and it was clear he didn't want guys messing with them—whether said guy was his best friend or not.

"You ready to get out of here?" Owen asked, already making his way to the front counter.

Rhys trailed behind. Even though he knew he shouldn't, he kept thinking of Avery, in a bikini, on the beach, with the sunscreen making her skin glisten in that totally irresistible way. And suddenly Rhys felt *very* excited.

Better run and get another pack of Magnums!

r is for . . . reunion

As would be expected on the day before Thanksgiving, JFK was a complete madhouse. Baby slouched in a ridiculously uncomfortable fake black leather seat by the gate. All morning, they'd waited at the penthouse for Layla's boyfriend, Riley, to join them. Apparently, the "bring a friend" policy extended to Remington's family too. Riley was driving in from upstate, but it had gotten so late, they'd decided to meet him at the airport. Remington's driver had expertly navigated through the ridiculous traffic, and the line for security was a mile long. Now they were finally at the gate, only to discover the plane was delayed.

Baby sighed. Airports were usually exciting; however, even though they were all heading off on an island vacation, no member of the Carlyle-Wallis party looked especially happy. Avery was sulking in a corner, obviously miffed that Jack had been unable to come and that they weren't taking a private plane. Owen and Rhys were both listening to their iPods, unaware of the all the girls passing by who stopped to give them second glances. Layla was furiously texting on her iPhone. Only Edie and Remington, their hands intertwined underneath a white cashmere throw, seemed to be in their own blissful world.

"I'm getting a magazine," Baby announced, even though no one was listening. She *hated* waiting. "Do you need anything?" She poked Layla hard on her bicep so that she looked up from her phone. Layla had been paranoid that Riley wouldn't make it in time. She'd told Baby that they met in high school and had been dating ever since, but because they went to different colleges, the holidays were one of the few times they got to spend more than a day or two together.

"No, I'm good. Riley just got through security, so he'll make it." Layla rolled her eyes good-naturedly. "Boys."

"I'm excited to meet him," Baby said agreeably. Hopefully, he'd be as cool as Layla, and hopefully they wouldn't mind her third-wheeling it with them. It wouldn't be long before she'd get sick of Avery's planned schedule of sunbathing, followed by spa treatments, followed by sessions of reading French *Vogue* by the pool, piña colada in hand. "Watch my stuff?" she asked, and Layla nodded.

Baby weaved her way around an overweight family of six, all wearing Mickey Mouse ears and sweatpants with Mickey's face emblazoned on the ass. She giggled, wishing she had someone to share this with. It was times like these, when she saw something absurd, that she wished she had a boyfriend—someone who'd understand what she was thinking. Still, it was probably for the best that she was single. After getting out of a long relationship with her high school boyfriend Tom, followed by a whirlwind affair with J. P. Cashman, Baby was fine just spending her vacation with her family, herself, and Nabokov.

Nothing like dark Russian novels to keep you warm at night.

Baby turned into the brightly lit Hudson Newsstand. Idly she scanned the racks, reaching for a copy of *Bitch* magazine. Sydney loved it, calling it feminism's answer to idiots. The cover was hot pink and had a picture of a Barbie doll–type figure on it. *Plastic Rocks!* read the white bubble-letter script. It did look kind of cool and subversive. Besides, if it was boring, she could always borrow one of her sister's five million fashion magazines. She pulled it off the shelf and headed toward the winding checkout line.

"Woah, *Bitch*. Should I be scared of you?"

Baby whirled around, expecting to see some asshole frat guy in an Abercrombie shirt. Instead, she saw a cute young guy wearing a vintage green ITHACA IS GORGES T-shirt, tightish black jeans, and dirty white Converses.

"No, but you should be scared of your own terrible conversation skills," Baby shot back.

"Sorry about that, it was supposed to be a joke. I hate how no one talks in airports, so sometimes I try to just say hi. In my own very lame way." The guy smiled sheepishly, shoving his hands in his pockets.

"Well, hi," Baby said shortly. She'd been expecting a confrontation, but he was so apologetic it caught her off guard. Baby turned back to the line. The girl in front of her had ripped open the bag of sunflower seeds she'd been holding, causing shells to scatter onto the floor.

"Need a snack?" The guy gestured toward the floor. "Just so you know," he said, leaning in confidentially, "I really like *Bitch*. Sometimes it gets a little too mired in third-wave feminism. I mean, you can really only read so many times about how Lindsay Lohan is an unlikely postmodern feminist poster girl, you know?" He shrugged and smiled, exposing brilliantly white teeth.

Baby narrowed her eyes. What was this guy's deal? She tried to get a clue from the magazines he was carrying: *Atlantic Monthly, Esquire, Vanity Fair.*

"Anyway, you'll like it," he encouraged, practically prying the magazine out of her hands. "Tell you what, since I was sort of lame, I'll buy it for you. Consider it an early Thanksgiving present."

"Thanks," Baby said, reevaluating the guy. So maybe he had a weird way of starting a conversation, but he seemed decent enough. And he was pretty cute in that kind of hipster-but-not-actually-trying sort of way. His dark hair was mussed but obviously product-free. "I should buy you something too," she decided. "In the spirit of reciprocity. Here . . ." She surveyed the store, her eyes falling on a shelf full of stuffed animals in front of the register.

"You have everything?" the bored-looking clerk asked.

"Just this!" Baby said, triumphantly plopping the fist-size, googly-eyed turkey down on the counter.

"No fair, you got to choose your present!" the boy objected. "I should get to pick mine." He turned to the clerk. "Actually, she wants this instead," he said, picking up a small snow globe from one of the glass kiosks surrounding the checkout. It had a tiny figurine of a penguin wearing a red sweater, standing in front of the Empire State Building.

"That's ugly." Baby wrinkled her nose.

"That's the point!" He plunked the snow globe down. "Besides, how often do you see a fashion-conscious penguin in the middle of Manhattan?" he teased.

Baby giggled as the checkout lady rolled her eyes and tapped her bright blue acrylic nails against the counter. "I don't have all day."

"We're good." Baby fished in her bag for a ten-dollar bill and passed it over to the woman.

"And I'd like *Bitch*, please," the guy said with a completely straight face. "The magazine!" He added quickly, pointing toward the title at the cashier's glare.

Laughing, they hurried out of the store.

"I'm glad you were there to protect me. I think she might have killed me," he said as he passed Baby the magazine.

"Those nails *were* pretty deadly," Baby agreed with a laugh. She handed him the tiny snow globe and he took it, their fingers lightly brushing at the exchange.

Baby stood there, looking into his hazel eyes. She knew she was supposed to say goodbye now . . . but the idea of walking back to the dreary waiting area alone felt oddly disappointing. "Well, good luck!" she said uncertainly, turning on her heel.

"Wait!" the guy sped up, keeping in step with her strides.

"Are you following me?" Baby challenged. She kind of wished he *was* following her. She realized the unsettled feeling in her stomach was butterflies. *That* was something she hadn't felt in a while.

"Depends on where you're headed." He arched a dark eyebrow.

Baby racked her brain for a flirty response but found herself coming up blank. "The Bahamas," she finally admitted.

"Me too." He broke into a large smile. "Gate thirty-eight?" he asked as they began walking together on the moving sidewalk.

"Yeah," Baby said happily as they approached the gate. So they wouldn't be parting ways anytime soon. "What seat are you?" she asked. Maybe they could trade with someone on the flight and sit next to each other. And how big was the Bahamas, anyway? Maybe they'd even be staying close by each other.

But he didn't seem to be paying attention. Instead, his hazel eyes were scanning the crowded waiting area, as if looking for someone.

"Riley!" Layla squealed, practically leaping from her seat and leaving both hers and Baby's things in a messy pile on the floor.

"Hey," he responded as Layla practically attacked him, wrapping him up in a hug.

Baby felt like she'd been drenched in a bucket of cold water. She turned away, staring at the line of planes ready to take off.

"Baby!" Layla called in her super-sweet voice. "Come meet the other half of Riled Up. Our band," she clarified. "This is Riley. And Riley, this is Baby, who's practically my new sister!"

"We've met," Baby said, shooting Riley a glance.

"We actually just met in the magazine stand," he explained, a little sheepishly. But Layla didn't seem to notice the embarrassed flush that was rising in his cheeks.

"Oh, cool. We're gonna have fun this week." Layla raised her eyebrows at both of them and Baby forced a smile back. The magazine suddenly felt heavy in her hand.

"Here, we can switch tickets so you and Layla can sit together." Baby coolly rummaged through her bag and yanked out her red ticket envelope. She ignored the hammering of her heart, instead concentrating on the small freckle at the top of Riley's left ear. It almost looked like an earring. She hadn't noticed that earlier, in the magazine stand.

Not that it mattered anymore.

up, up and away

"Hey, it's Avery. Our plane's delayed, so I just wanted to say there's still time to come with us if you change your mind. Apparently Layla's bringing her boyfriend." Avery lowered her voice into her phone as she continued her message on Jack's voice mail. Just a few feet away Layla was practically smothering a gangly, dark-haired boy. Um, get a room?

"Anyway, call me back if you get this." Avery flipped her phone closed and walked toward the corner of the gate, far enough away from what seemed to be a Neil Diamond fan club, but close enough to hear boarding announcements. Hopefully, first class would be called soon. It was weird how Remington didn't just have them wait in the Admiral's Club or whatever, but it was probably just because he was traveling with six teenagers, like some sitcom.

The Spoiled Bunch?

"Oh, there you are, darling!" Her mom was wearing a large straw hat paired with a black wrap dress and multicolored leggings. "I know I'm being a mother hen, but I just want to make sure we all get on the plane together," she fretted.

"No worries," Avery said agreeably. She slid her phone into her Marc by Marc Jacobs straw tote and dutifully followed her mom back to the entire row she'd commandeered with her mismatched collection of hemp bags.

"Rows thirty-seven through fifty can board now," intoned the screechy intercom voice. Instantly, people sprang to attention, as if the plane was about to take off immediately.

"That's us, troops!" Remington announced, slapping his hands against his knees and pulling himself to a standing position. He wore a pair of white linen pants and a white linen shirt, looking sort of like a monk. It was obvious Edie had picked out his outfit.

"Really?" Avery asked in disbelief. They were flying *coach*? She hoped Remington was pulling one of those goofy-dad jokes. But he was leading Edie by the hand to the gate. "What?" Avery said, again, loudly. Owen walked by and offered a half-shrug, not bothering to take off his headphones.

"I'm going to be sick," Avery announced loudly to no one in particular as she walked down the Jetway. Not like she was being snobby, but Remington used to own an *island*! He gave away millions of dollars every year to fund art projects consisting of weird, ugly sculptures displayed in Brooklyn, and he couldn't spring for first class?

Better hope she doesn't get a middle seat!

Avery spotted Baby a few feet in front of her, holding a magazine open with her index finger. Avery sped up, wanting to commiserate with her sister. But instead of stopping, Baby marched quickly down the Jetway and through the tiny doorway of the plane.

"Ticket?" the perky blond flight attendant asked, stopping Avery.

"He has them." Avery jutted her chin toward Remington.

"Great! Just keep walking back!" The flight attendant flashed an ultra-fake smile as Avery stepped into the tiny cabin of the plane, which had three-seat rows on one side and two-seat rows on the other. It smelled like unwashed socks and wet wool.

Ahead of her, Owen and Rhys were immersed in conversation, and Baby wordlessly sank into her window seat next to Layla. Layla's boyfriend was kind of cute in that sort of pretentious intellectual way that Baby always loved. But instead of hanging out with Layla and her boyfriend, Baby had her arms crossed over her chest, her large vintage purple aviators pulled over her eyes. Weird. Maybe she was annoyed about the plane situation too.

Avery glanced down at her ticket stub. If Rhys and Owen were in one of the double seats, and Baby, Layla, and her boyfriend were in one of the three-seat rows, who was *she* seated next to?

"Are we neighbors?" Remington boomed from the row ahead. His six-foot-two frame was uncomfortably folded into the middle seat. Avery looked down and saw that she was assigned to the aisle seat next to him, her mother already seated by the window. *Great.*

"Avery, I'm going to ask you to show some mercy on me. Switch?" he asked sheepishly, looking up from the clutter of Bose headphones, his BlackBerry, and a copy of the book *The Fat Man in History*. Avery hoped it was a metaphor and not some fetish or hobby.

She nodded, her stomach sinking. It wasn't *her* fault Remington couldn't fit into his airplane seat. Already, this trip hadn't quite lived up to her expectations.

"Thank you." Remington shuffled into the aisle to allow Avery room to squeeze into the ultra-cramped row.

"Why are we traveling like this?" Avery whispered urgently as she poked her mom in her yoga-toned bicep. Edie flipped up the lilac-colored organic-fabric eye mask she was wearing.

"Well, it's not a long trip. I was looking online, and do you *know* the carbon footprint produced by just *one* private flight?" Edie's eyes widened in disbelief.

"I don't care," Avery said sulkily, looking straight ahead at the ugly pattern of the seat fabric in front of her. Couldn't they just, like, donate money to some carbon emissions fund?

"Besides, this is fun! Why be elitist?" Edie shook her head wildly as if to shake off the very idea. "I'm just going to sleep anyway." She flipped the eyeshade back over her eyes and leaned back with a contented sigh.

"A woman of many talents." Remington nodded fondly over at Edie, who seemed to have already fallen asleep. She let out little birdlike whistles as she exhaled.

"Yep," Avery muttered. She pulled a copy of *Vogue* from her bag and flipped it open. *Skirts, skirts, skirts!* The text swam in front of her. All she wanted to do this week was spend as much time as possible in her bikini, anyway. She couldn't wait to get out on the beach, margarita in hand, Bumble and Bumble surf spray tucked into her straw tote.

The guy in front of her pushed his seat into a reclining position, bumping Avery's knees. Avery accidentally-on-purpose banged her knee against the seat in annoyance and let out a loud sigh. Was it so important for him to recline *right this second*?

She closed her eyes again as the engine whirred to life beneath them. She was always a little nervous about flying, and usually had to close her eyes and imagine something relaxing. Usually she thought of a Nantucket sunset, or a perfectly organized walk-in closet. Now, though, an image of Rhys sprang into her mind. Would he wear board shorts or Speedos on the beach? Speedos were sort of gross, but according to Owen, it was like a badge of honor for the swim team guys to wear their Speedos wherever and whenever possible. Owen used to wear them instead of boxers under his jeans on meet days back in Nantucket. Still, the idea of seeing Rhys in a Speedo made her feel shy and excited at the same time.

So much for relaxing.

Avery opened her eyes and flipped through her magazine. At least this was a short flight. "A drink, miss?" A spiky-haired, super-skinny male flight attendant looked down at her.

"Tea with lemon, two Splendas," Avery rattled off, looking guiltily at Remington. She really wanted to order a well-deserved *I'm on vacation* vodka tonic, but she couldn't risk Remington thinking she was an alcoholic or something.

"Hmmm, well, we have sugar, no Splenda. And we don't have lemon." The steward shrugged, triumphantly handing her a tiny Styrofoam cup. "Pretzels?"

"Do you have any fruit? Or a yogurt?" Avery asked, wrinkling her nose.

"This isn't a restaurant," the steward responded loudly. "Here's another pack of pretzels. I normally only give people one pack."

"Thanks." Avery rolled her eyes as she gazed down at the two small foil packages the steward had flung on the plastic Formica tray in front of her.

"I saw that eye-roll, young lady." Remington closed his hands over her pretzels. He raised a salt-and-pepper eyebrow at her.

"Sorry," Avery huffed, feeling embarrassed but annoyed. Yeah, she was being a brat, and she knew it. But the fact that her mom had found someone with the same hippie-ish ideals as her made for a lot of craptastic experiences to come. She'd hoped Remington's banker past would make for a cushy future, but apparently he was as annoyingly eco-chic as her mom.

"I haven't flown coach since eighty-eight," Remington whispered confidentially. "But I thought ahead." He leaned down and pulled a white-and-orange paper bag from his briefcase. "I've got bagels with chive cream cheese or lemon-zest scones. Your choice."

"Oh my God, thanks." Avery gratefully grabbed a slightly crumbled scone from the bag, instantly feeling better.

"I had my assistant get them this morning. I wish I could also get my assistant to persuade your mother to take my plane." He shook his head ruefully, glancing over at a sleeping Edie. Her mouth was half open, her head resting against the window.

"Your plane?" Avery raised one blond eyebrow. So Remington hadn't totally lost touch with his former luxe lifestyle.

You never *can* go back.

"Yep." Remington sighed as he pulled a bagel out from the bag and placed it on his own tray. "Maybe you can help persuade your mom to take it on the way back? I'm not doing this again." Remington grinned as he took a bite of bagel.

"Sure." Avery nodded and smiled. It was so obvious that Remington was head over heels in *love* with her mother. It made her feel weird, but not for the reasons she'd thought it would. She honestly didn't mind the fact that her mom was with a guy. What made her feel weird was wondering whether she'd *ever* feel that way about anyone.

She glanced across the aisle. Rhys was hunched down over his iPod, his dark hair falling over his forehead. Avery quickly looked away, back down at her magazine, concentrating on her relaxing vision of the waves lapping the beach in Nantucket as the plane took off.

Across the aisle, Owen shifted in his seat, trying to get comfortable. He must have grown since the last time he'd flown coach, because his knees were banging into the blue seat in front of him. The plane was full, and he could just make out the dark tangle of Baby's hair several rows ahead. Why was she sitting up there, with Remington's daughter and her hipster boyfriend? It was as if they'd totally infiltrated their family.

"Do you think Baby's okay?" Owen asked Rhys, nodding ahead.

"Huh?" Rhys glanced up from his iPod. He'd downloaded a season of *Lost,* but he had no idea what the fuck was going on.

"What is Remington's deal? Why is, like, his entire extended family coming on this trip? Can't he just chill out?" Owen leaned back in his seat, jabbing his knees against the seat in front of him.

"Hey!" A fat, red-faced man wearing an ill-fitting Yankees cap on his almost-bald head turned around and glared at Owen.

"Sorry, man." Owen shook his head. He took a sip of orange juice from the Styrofoam cup on the plastic tray in front of him. It sucked that the flight attendant had been such a hard-ass about alcohol. A couple mini bottles of vodka sounded *really* good right about now.

"Dude, you want to talk?" Rhys pulled off his Bose headphones and glanced pointedly at his friend. He'd never seen Owen like this, and while a tiny part of him was sort of happy to see Carlyle being less than perfect, the other, *better* part of him wanted to help his buddy out.

"Sorry, I'll chill." Owen unclenched his jaw. For as long as he remembered, it had always been the triplets and their mom. Now, all of a sudden, this guy was telling them where to vacation and how to get there. What the fuck?. "It's just, they just started dating, and all of a sudden, we're going on a family vacation. I feel like the next thing they'll do is get married." A shiver ran down Owen's spine. *Would* they get married?

What happens in the Bahamas, stays in the Bahamas. . . .

Rhys shrugged. "Dude, I know, it sucks. But maybe he'll be cool once you get to know him," he offered lamely.

"Yeah." Owen didn't want to talk about Remington anymore. "Anyway, who cares, right? Fuck it," he said with false conviction. "We'll just do our own thing this weekend. Aka getting *laid*," Owen finished.

The spiky-haired steward who'd refused to serve them alcohol stopped mid-step and glared at them. "Please keep your voices down—some of our passengers are trying to sleep," he hissed as he pushed his beverage cart further down the aisle.

"Sorry." Owen shrugged.

"I can't wait to meet some new girls," Rhys said a little unconvincingly. He couldn't stop sneaking glances toward Avery, who looked hot even when she was smushed into the middle seat, in coach.

"Yeah, man. It's going to be legendary!" Owen nodded. He needed to forget about his mom and her freaky-ass boyfriend. There was work to be done: His buddy *needed* to lose his V card.

Ever since Owen and Kelsey had broken up, things had been *almost* back to normal between him and Rhys. But there were still tense moments, like when the topic of sex came up in the locker room, or Hugh Moore made some inappropriate comment about the time Rhys had walked in on Owen and Kelsey together. But if Owen helped Rhys find someone to lose it to, they could put it all behind them. They'd be on the same page, ready to go back to New York as equals. It was the perfect plan.

As long as it doesn't become a *family* plan.

j needs a challenge

Jack strode into Barneys later that morning, her brand-new only-available-in-France five-inch black suede Christian Louboutin ankle booties—which her mother had shipped to her in a fit of obvious maternal guilt—clacking loudly against the ultra-polished floor. Even though it was only 11 a.m., the aisles around the handbag displays surrounding the entrance were already buzzing with Eurotrashy tourists.

She ignored the Balenciaga and Marc Jacobs displays and confidently made a left toward the elevator bank. She was on a mission, and that mission was to get ready for Operation: *Do It*, tomorrow night.

Jack pushed the button firmly with her petal-polished finger. Now that she'd finally gotten her credit cards back from her father, after an embarrassing three months of being cut off, she had to make up for lost time. And of course, she'd come to Barneys, her favorite place on earth. When Jack was in fourth grade, she'd written a report on the children's book *From the Mixed-Up Files of Mrs. Basil E. Frankweiler*, which was all about two kids who stay overnight in the Metropolitan Museum of Art. Jack had written about how much *better* it would have been if the kids had spent the night in Barneys. The fourth-grade teacher, Mrs. Gherke, whom everyone called Mrs. Jerk and whose hair was always styled in a dykey bowl cut, had made her redo the report. But sometimes Jack still wished she could get trapped at Barneys overnight.

The door to the elevator opened and Jack stepped on, squeezing between several women wearing fur coats that doubled their body mass. Just as she pressed the door-closed button, two girls run-walked up to the elevator and shoved on.

"Hey! You're here. Why didn't you tell us where you were?" Genevieve demanded. Jack could smell smoke on her breath.

"I thought we were meeting outside," Jiffy seconded. "Even though it's freezing." She theatrically pulled off her purple leather motorcycle gloves and blew on her fingers for warmth.

"Sorry, guys. I forgot," Jack said coolly, appraising her two friends. In truth, she wasn't sure why she'd invited Genevieve and Jiffy to come with her. It wasn't as if underwear shopping was exactly a group activity. Of course, back when they were thirteen or fourteen, they used to spend hours looking at the underwear displays at Barneys, daring each other to actually buy a La Perla bra or Cosabella thong. But now it was real.

And even more fun than dress-up!

"Obviously, you're nervous," Genevieve said condescendingly as she marched off the elevator and made a beeline for the rows of underwear and bras.

"Thanks," Jack said shortly, resisting the very immature desire to stick her tongue out at Genevieve's back. Genevieve had lost her virginity to some C-list teen actor a couple weeks ago, when she'd been visiting her director dad in L.A. over Columbus Day weekend for the Teen Choice Awards. She was the first of Jack's friends to have had sex and wouldn't let the rest of them forget it.

"So you're really going to do it?" Jiffy asked loudly, stopping by a collection of ugly pink-and-black lace demi-bras.

"Can I help you ladies?" a saleswoman asked, smoothly stepping in between Jiffy and the display. From her tone of voice, it was clear she wanted to kick them upstairs to the Co-op to giggle over Marc Jacobs handbags.

"No, we're fine." Jack stalked over to a collection of soft cashmere pajama pants. They were boring, but at least she'd be out of the nosy saleslady's earshot.

"Honestly, I think lingerie is passé." Genevieve sighed loudly as she gestured around the room. "I mean, it's all coming off anyway. You should, like, come to the door just wearing a strategically tied bow. They have these really big gold ones at Kate's Paperie. It'd be so sexy, because he'd be, like, unwrapping you."

Jack glared at her friend. *Unwrapping* her? Was she serious?

She wandered over to a round, glass-covered display table and fingered a light blue bra and panty set. It was cute, but did it look too much like a bikini? She closed her eyes and tried to imagine her and J.P. finally doing it. She would play music, maybe something jazzy and Nina Simone–esque. And maybe she'd light candles, or set up some low, figure-flattering lighting. Strawberries and champagne were a must. But should she go slutty or girly? Cover up or show it all? Why was this so *hard*?

Jiffy sidled up to her, carrying an ugly peach-colored camisole on a light pink padded hanger. "You should wear this, with just your pointe shoes. Doesn't every guy have a ballerina fantasy?" she asked eagerly.

"That's gross," Jack said shortly. At this point, she'd rather have gone shopping with the stepbrats than with her friends. "Look, I'll meet you and Gen somewhere. I just need to concentrate."

"I thought you wanted us to come with you." Hurt registered in Jiffy's pert, freckly face.

"Jif, let's go." Genevieve called from across the room, causing the saleslady to glare angrily at her. "If Jack doesn't need our help, she doesn't need it. Besides, J.P.'s the only one who matters. And he'll love it. After all, you're having *sex* with him!" she called over her shoulder, just to piss Jack off.

"Shut up!" Jack hissed, feeling her face turn bright red. She didn't usually get embarrassed, but she was in her favorite department store, surrounded by her two immature friends screaming about sex.

Just then, a group of loud, chattering girls burst into the otherwise quiet corner of the floor.

"It's her hen party!" one of the girls exclaimed in a burry Scottish accent, gesturing to a tall, curly-haired girl with bad skin. "We want her to get all tarted up, then we're going to Marquee!" she added, pleased to share her news with anyone who would listen. Jiffy nodded eagerly, obviously wanting to be part of an underwear-shopping experience more like that one.

Jack rolled her eyes. The girl who was getting married—the *hen*?—was sort of chunky and had bad teeth, but she looked radiant and happy. Jack imagined having her own bachelorette party, surrounded by Jiffy and Genevieve. They'd laugh as they looked back on this day, which by then would seem ridiculously far in the past. But she couldn't quite conjure up the image. If she was getting overwhelmed just thinking about *sex* with J.P., how were they ever going to get *married*? Jack took a deep breath and tried to focus on the task in front of her. It was just underwear. It was just sex. It was just J.P., her loving, caring boyfriend. "*Perfect*," she chanted quietly to herself, her own personal mantra.

Usually, she said it when things weren't perfect at all.

"I need to go," she announced. But Genevieve and Jiffy were giggling along with the Scottish girls, not even listening to her.

Fuck this. She'd just go and buy underwear *by herself*, which she should have done in the first place. Maybe at La Petite Coquette, that adorable store in the village. Somewhere quiet, discreet, where people weren't haranguing her about ballerina fantasies or shrieking about their tacky weddings. Somewhere she could just plan her special day with J.P. and *not* freak the fuck out. Jack stormed back to the elevator and pressed the down button, anxious to get downstairs and out of Barneys.

Isn't she glad she doesn't live there now?

vacation, all a ever wanted

Avery peeled her avocado green Milly cardigan off her shoulders as she exited the tiny North Eleuthera airport. Behind them, a porter was busily pushing a cart piled high with Avery's Louis Vuitton luggage and Edie's army green duffel.

"How was your flight?" Rhys asked shyly, coming up alongside Avery. He was still wearing his black Ralph Lauren sweater and his pressed khakis, small beads of sweat forming at his hairline.

"All right," Avery said as she pushed her Coach sunglasses on top of her wheat blond hair. *All right?* How lame was she? She felt like she'd been chewing on an old sock. She took a small tin of Altoid mints out of her tote. "Want one?" she offered.

"Sure." Rhys grabbed two mints and crunched them between his front teeth.

"Wallis party?" an elderly man asked, opening the door to a stretch SUV. Avery smiled in satisfaction. She'd been worried that this would be one of those totally gross back-to-the-elements vacations where people paid thousands to hike in a desert and stay in a yurt. But the SUV looked appropriately luxurious.

"This is lovely," Edie cooed, apparently not doing the math

on the SUV's carbon footprint. She'd removed her leg warmers and was wearing a pair of ugly earth-friendly straw sandals. "Remington, thank you!" Edie flung her arms around Remington's neck and kissed him.

"Mom," Avery hissed. The PDAs *had* to stop.

"You kids." Edie shook her head. Over by the curb, Layla and Riley were holding hands, while Baby sat on her duffel, hugging her knees. This was the weirdest group of people ever. Before, Carlyle family vacations had consisted of visiting Edie's far-flung friends or tagging along with their grandmother Avery on one of her intercontinental adventures. One year, they'd helped make hammocks at a self-sustaining Vermont commune. Another, Avery had gone on a Mediterranean cruise with Grandmother Avery and had been the youngest on the ship by at least fifty years.

"We're in the back!" Layla giggled, ducking into the SUV. Avery carefully climbed into the car. Once the bags were situated, the SUV lurched away from the airport, turning onto a dirt road that hugged the coast. The island was about an hour's drive away, separated from the mainland by a causeway.

"You okay?" Baby whispered to her sister. Avery nodded. Usually she got sort of carsick, unless she focused on one particular thing that wasn't moving. Now she found herself focusing on the back of Rhys's neck. It was a nice neck—not too skinny, but not too thick, with a couple of freckles in an uneven starlike constellation.

Finally, the car rolled up a dirt road and stopped at a cluster of glass-walled villas surrounded by palm trees on one side, the ocean on the other. Shelter Cay was a ten-square-mile property that held a private resort with adjacent villas, along with a few privately owned cottages. The villas were connected by a wrap-around birchwood deck, and the sliding doors were flung open, the organic-cotton curtains blowing in the slight breeze. Avery sucked in her breath happily. This was where they were *staying*?

"We're here, guys!" Remington boomed. "You can put the bags there," he directed the driver. "What do you think?" he asked, winking at Avery. Avery smiled giddily back. Her luck was finally changing.

"Okay, troops. So, you ladies can stay here, the guys can go over to the villa on the left, and your mom and I will be in the back," Remington commanded. "Go out and explore!"

Avery made her way into the girls' villa. It was bright and airy, and only had three walls, the fourth looking out to a large swimming pool and the beach below. There were three single beds in the master bedroom, and a large sitting room, where a bottle of champagne was nestled in a sterling silver bucket.

Bottoms up!

"Cheers!" Avery announced, holding up the bottle. She put it between her knees and expertly popped the cork, the champagne releasing a spray on the bamboo floors. She felt a little giddy already.

"I need a glass," Baby announced.

"Make that two!" Layla yelled, emerging from the master bedroom. Avery glanced up. Layla was standing in her underwear, her impossibly perky 34B chest on display. A tiny gold ring dangled from her belly button, but it was so small it looked cute rather than skanky. She ducked down and rifled through her oversize camouflage duffel bag that was flung on the floor, triumphantly pulling out a tiny white string bikini.

"Baby, can you help me tie this?" Layla called. "Riley and I always go horseback riding as soon as we get here. I'm not big on riding, but there's this really cool beach on the other side of the island. You girls want to come?" She smiled sweetly. She had a tribal tattoo around her skinny bicep. Even *that* was cute.

"Don't you want to unpack?" Avery wrinkled her nose. They'd only been here for five minutes, and it already looked like a bomb had exploded in the bedroom.

"We're on vacation! Ignore my anal sister." Baby rolled her eyes at Layla. "I'll come," she said, plunking down her champagne glass on the marble counter of the kitchenette. She'd spent a lot of time thinking on the drive over, and was annoyed with herself for acting so sulky earlier. Sure, she'd thought Riley was cute in the magazine stand, and it was kind of disappointing to realize he hadn't been flirting with her at all, just being friendly. But it was a two-second crush, and no good reason to ruin her vacation. Layla was cool, Riley seemed cool, and Baby was going to just chill out too. She loved horseback riding, and wasn't about to pass up the opportunity.

She took off her own Brooklyn Industries T-shirt, displaying her skinny rib cage and a black bra.

"Guys!" Avery screeched, pulling the curtains closed. Layla and Baby didn't seem to care that anyone walking by could see them.

Half-naked peas in a pod.

"Lighten up, we're in the islands!" Baby called, rifling through Avery's suitcase, knowing that'd *really* annoy her sister.

"You better not take anything with a tag on it," Avery allowed, glancing over Baby's shoulder. "And be *careful*," she added as Baby haphazardly threw a white 3.1 by Phillip Lim dress on the floor.

"You guys are so funny." Layla laughed at their sisterly banter. "Sometimes I wish I weren't an only child." She smiled at Baby. "Ready?"

"You sure you don't want to come, Ave?" Baby asked.

"No thanks." Avery finished off her champagne. Horses were dirty and smelly. Not her idea of a tropical getaway.

"Fine." Baby stuck out her tongue and followed Layla out the door.

Avery poured another glass of champagne and walked around the villa. She carefully pulled her clothes out of her suitcase, shaking them slightly. Unlike Baby, neatness was important to her. Before she could even think about exploring, she needed to have bathing suits in one drawer, tank tops in another, and dresses hung in the expansive walk-in closet.

Once her sandals were neatly arranged in the closet, her bathing suits stacked according to their appropriateness for the beach versus the pool, and the champagne half-gone, Avery felt like she was *really* on vacation. She pulled a billowy magenta Calypso dress over her head and smiled at the mirror in satisfaction. It was the type of dress that looked shapeless on the hanger but amazing on. Especially since she'd sneaked in a scrub and color appointment at Bliss early this morning, and her skin already had a summery-bronze glow.

She stepped onto the balcony, still holding her champagne glass. There was a soft breeze, and in the distance she could make out the thatched roofs of other villas. But it felt extremely private where they were, as if they were marooned on a totally fabulous tropical island. Manhattan seemed very far away.

"Hey!"

Avery whirled around. Standing there, wearing a white linen

button-down shirt and khaki shorts, was Rhys, Ray-Ban aviators on his head.

"Hi." Avery bit her coral-colored lip, suddenly shy. She gripped the hand railing.

"Owen went for a run and Riley went horseback riding or something," Rhys explained. "I stuck around unpacking. Besides, I sort of like to forget the exercise routine when I'm on vacation." He shrugged. "What are you up to?"

"I don't know." Avery cringed. Another brilliant line. "Want a glass?" She held up her own empty glass. Oops. When did that happen?

Somewhere in between stacking sandals and color-coding camis.

"I'm okay. We opened our champagne too." Rhys smiled and rested his hands against the deck railing. "You know, I totally owe your brother. If he hadn't invited me, I'd be foxhunting right now."

"Really?" Avery giggled. She knew Rhys's parents were British, but *foxhunting*? Actually, after watching *Tea with Lady Sterling*, she could sort of believe it. Most of the time, the show was over-the-top, even for her. But her stomach leapt every time Lady Sterling mentioned Rhys's name.

"Actually, it's brutal. A bit worse for the foxes, though," Rhys allowed. "What about you? Do you guys have any weird family traditions?"

"Not really," Avery lied. She was *not* going to talk about how her mom used to make the triplets recite poetry or do weird interpretive dances at her dinner parties.

"Your whole family seems so cool," Rhys continued. "You're lucky. I always wanted a brother or sister." He shrugged, and

Avery followed his gaze out to the ocean, wanting to see what he was seeing. She could just make out tiny boats bobbing on the robin's egg blue ocean. It was the exact color of a Tiffany box. It almost didn't look real.

"It's so beautiful," Avery murmured.

"Want to go for a walk and explore? I haven't been to the beach in forever, unless you count Bournemouth, which I don't." Rhys rolled his eyes.

"Sure." Avery smiled.

"Here." He held her arm as he helped her down the limestone steps that led from the terrace down a hillside and toward the beach. He pulled his sunglasses over his eyes. "Which way?"

"Left," Avery decided. The sun was setting to the left, casting a romantic, orangish glow over the water.

"That was my choice too. Anyway, I'm so glad Owen invited me. He's a great friend. Especially now that . . ." Rhys trailed off, a cloud passing over his brown eyes. Avery had a feeling he was thinking of his ex, Kelsey. That whole love triangle was so weird, and she was glad it seemed to be in the past now. The not-so-distant past, apparently, but maybe being on vacation would take Rhys's mind off it. "Well, he's just cool," Rhys finished lamely.

"He wasn't always," Avery confided. "He used to torture Baby and me when we were little. He went through one phase, when we were five or six, where he used to collect sand crabs and put them in our beds." She blushed as the words left her mouth. *Crabs in her bed?* Could she have thought of a more embarrassing conversation topic?

Only time will tell. . . .

"Really? That asshole! Like this one?" Rhys bent down toward the water and plucked a tiny crab from the marble-colored sand. Its little legs desperately clawed the air.

"Ewww!" Avery giggled as she ran down the beach, loving the feeling of her hair whipping against her face. She suddenly remembered what it was like as a little kid, playing by the ocean back in Nantucket. She wasn't worried if her boobs were bouncing or her dress was in danger of slipping off her shoulders, or even if she was getting salt water on her new dress. Instead, she just felt free, in a way she hadn't since arriving in New York.

"Okay. He's gone!" Rhys called, easily jogging up to her. "Truce?" He held up his hands to prove that he wasn't carrying any crabs.

"Truce!" Avery giggled. She wasn't sure if it was the sunset or the champagne or just the easy way Rhys wasn't afraid to tease her, but suddenly, Avery didn't feel shy anymore. "Until I get revenge," she added, grinning.

"Yeah? It's on." Rhys grabbed Avery's hand and goofily shook it.

Avery slowly, reluctantly, took her hand out of his. "Low tide," she noted. The sand stretched for what seemed like miles into the horizon. Back in Nantucket, knowing the tide was as second nature as breathing.

"Should we sit for a bit?" Rhys suggested.

"Sure." Avery smoothed out a spot of sand with her hands.

"Wait!" Rhys pulled off his shirt and set it on the sand. "We can sit on this." He had a defined six-pack and his chest had a slight hint of a tan.

Seems like two people just missed each other at Bliss this morning!

Just then, a buzzing sounded from the front pocket of the shirt. Avery glanced down in confusion.

"Phone," Rhys explained hastily as he quickly yanked it out of the pocket. He *really* hoped it wasn't his mom. He pulled out his iPhone and glanced at the display.

U a man yet? Remember, chicks love sunsets, champagne, and private beaches. Consider this ur tip of the day.

Hugh. Rhys blushed. It felt really romantic being here with Avery, but Hugh's texts made him feel like he was just putting the moves on her.

"Your phone works here?" Avery asked in surprise.

"Yeah, sorry. I'm turning it off." Rhys firmly pressed the power button. He sat down in the sand, aware of Avery's hip brushing his. All he wanted to do was sit here and relax, not think about Hugh's playboy suggestions. Why had he even agreed to this absurd virginity-losing plan? This wasn't some comedy starring Seth Rogen, it was his *life*. And when it came to Avery, sex was out of the question. She was Owen's sister. And now that he and Owen were closer than ever, the last thing he wanted was to jeopardize their friendship by going for Avery.

Avery lay back, her stomach neatly concaving from her ribs. She cutely sprawled her arms out in the sand, like she was making a sand angel. Rhys resisted the urge to take her hand or kiss her. Avery wasn't the type of girl you lost your virginity to. She was too beautiful and precious and special. For now, they should just stay friends. They could do that, right?

Right.

animal attraction

"Slow down! I swear to God, he always does this to freak me out!" Layla yelled as Riley slammed his foot against the gas pedal of the Gator golf cart that came with each villa.

"Layla has issues with rough riding," Riley yelled. The wind was whipping his longish brown hair. "You okay, Baby?"

"Beats a cab!" Baby grinned, glad she'd decided to tag along. Layla and Riley had been joke-fighting the entire ride, but at least they weren't an ultra-gross PDA couple who sucked face in front of her all the time.

On their left, an identical golf cart filled with sunburned guys in their twenties chugged up beside them. "Backseat betties, nice job, man!" one of the guys called approvingly to Riley.

Baby stuck out her tongue flirtily. Instantly Riley hit the gas, zooming away from the other cart and taking a tight turn on the lush green path.

"Ow!" Baby cried as her hip slammed into the side of the molded plastic seats.

"Sorry 'bout that," Riley said, not sounding sorry at all. "I just didn't want to share you girls."

"Riley, is that how you and all your player friends talk at school?" Layla turned to Baby. "His new band is called the Players. I think they let their name get to their heads," Layla rolled her large green eyes. From her tone, it was hard to tell whether she was joking or not.

"So I think we'll have fun riding. I'm awful, but Riley's amazing. When we came last year, he was practically hired by the stables. He grew up in Texas and has been riding horses since forever." Layla smiled proudly, two dimples appearing on her cheeks.

Baby nodded, glancing over at Riley as he drummed his fingers on the steering wheel in some private rhythm. She'd noticed calluses on his hands and had assumed they were from playing the guitar. But maybe there was more to him than the musician-type she'd seen so far.

Finally, they pulled up to a slate-gray stable next to the beach. Unlike the rest of the property, which was filled with palapa-leaf thatched roofs, infinity swimming pools, and slate floors, the stables looked ramshackle and pleasantly weather-beaten, as if they'd been there long before the villas.

"Welcome back!" A woman in her twenties ran out from the stables, her long black hair trailing behind her. "I'm Erika," she introduced herself to Baby, after giving both Layla and Riley hugs.

"So, what's your riding experience?" she asked Baby.

"I took lessons when I was younger, but I haven't ridden in years." Baby had always loved horses and had begged her mom for lessons when she was thirteen. But she'd been so disappointed by how many rules there were, how much supervision, and how slowly you had to go at first—she'd wanted to just ride free. Eventually she'd given it up.

"Okay, we'll call you a beginner, just to play it safe. I'll get you some appropriate horses. Riley, will you help me?" She turned around and walked back to the stable.

A few minutes later Riley emerged from the stables with two horses, followed by Erika. "Okay. Layla, you've got Dusty, the developmentally challenged, super-slow pony, and I've got my girl, Nikita." He turned to Baby.

"Erika set you up with Birdie. She's sort of a wild card," he warned. Erika handed Baby the worn leather reins, at the end of which was a dappled mare, who snorted loudly. "Need a boost?"

Baby nodded as Riley bent down and formed an impromptu step stool with his hands. He smelled like leather and sunscreen, and Baby's stomach did an involuntary flip. Instead she focused on mounting Birdie. She was shorter than most people, but she hadn't remembered horses being so *big*. Gently, Baby stepped her Puma sneaker on Riley's palms and swung her leg over the horse.

"Hey," Baby whispered into Birdie's straw-colored mane. The horse whinnied loudly. Behind her, Layla was laughing as she struggled onto her own horse. It was so cool how Layla could laugh at herself like that, without seeming at all self-conscious or insecure. Instead, Layla just seemed to take life's adventures as they came, without worrying too much what people thought of her or what she looked like. Just like Baby.

"Okay, let's go!" Riley whooped.

"C'mon girl," Baby whispered, squeezing the sides of the horse gently with her inner thighs. It was weird how quickly it came back to her what to do. The horse took off, carefully plodding around the stables and down the beach.

"Um, does this thing come with keys?" Layla called. Her horse was standing still, as if unsure what to do with itself.

"Here!" Erika came up to the horse and slapped it. Suddenly, it took off down the beach.

"Woah, thanks, E!" Riley called, laughing as he took off down the beach after Layla and Dusty.

Baby slowly trailed behind as her horse navigated its way down the beach. Once on the sand, it made its way toward the shoreline, hugging the water. Baby started to relax as she got the hang of riding.

"Hey!" Riley had circled back and now he cantered up next to her. "She's being gentle with you," he noted as both horses fell into step and, as if on cue, turned toward the greenish-blue surf. It looked nothing like the Nantucket ocean, where even on the nicest days the water was an ominous navy blue. Here, the water was a bright, gorgeous turquoise, sparkling and full of promise.

"Tell the horse not to go into the water!" Layla shouted as Riley and Baby's horses easily moved past her, a note of panic in her voice.

"You tell him. With your thighs!" Riley yelled back, cracking a smile.

"I'd rather tell *you*," Layla shouted back. "This horse is not a good listener!" Her voice carried on the wind.

"Should we wait for her?" Baby asked.

"She's fine," Riley said to Baby as their horses walked along the shore. Already the sun was setting. Baby sucked in her breath. *This* was her idea of paradise.

She closed her eyes for a moment, loving that she could feel the orangey glow of the sun through her closed eyelids. The waves were gently lapping toward the horses' ankles, occasionally sending tiny sprays of salt water onto Baby's legs. Nothing felt more natural to her than being by the ocean, and she was glad that Riley seemed to understand that. They rode on for a little in silence, toward the sunset. Even though they weren't talking, Baby felt strangely comfortable.

Finally, Riley broke the silence. "So, tell me, Baby . . ."

Baby sighed, knowing he was about to ask her where she got her name. Everyone did, sooner or later. She didn't blame them, but it was kind of annoying to always have to explain how her mom had never bothered with an ultrasound and had thought she was having twins until the triplets were born. Owen and Avery were named after their grandparents, while the third birth certificate had simply read *Baby*. The name stuck.

Baby opened her mouth to explain, but Riley cut her off. "Two truths and a lie. Go."

"Me?" Baby asked, surprised.

"No, your horse." Riley rolled his hazel eyes as he easily led his horse into a gallop. "Come on!"

Baby grinned as she dug her heels into Birdie's sides, gently but hard enough that the horse broke into a gallop. They chased Riley and his horse, Nikita, down the beach, kicking up sand as they went. Baby loved the feel of the salty air whipping through her hair and against her skin.

She quickly caught up with Riley, and he looked surprised as she drew up beside him. Baby shot him a *don't underestimate me* look, and Riley raised an eyebrow, impressed. He slowed his horse to a walk, and Baby did the same.

"I'm sixteen, I used to have an imaginary friend named Estella, and I have a boyfriend," Baby said, the two truths and a lie coming out before she'd even really thought them through. She didn't know why she'd used the lame boyfriend lie.

Perhaps to let a certain someone know she's single?

"Hmmm," Riley considered. The ocean breeze ruffled his thick dark hair. "You're lying about your age. You're really twenty-five and just play the naïve high schooler to get attention."

Baby shook her head and grinned.

"Well, everyone has an imaginary friend when they're little, so I guess you have to be single." His eyes looked hopeful as he took Baby in. "Right?" He blushed a little and turned forward, speeding up slightly.

"Maybe yes, maybe no." Baby cringed as soon as she said it. That was not what she should have said. She sounded so *flirty*. But there was just something about Riley that made it impossible for her to think straight.

Riley guided his horse away from the beach and into a densely canopied trail. "We're heading to the other side of the island," he explained as Baby and her horse caught up to him on the path. "That wasn't a very good two truths and a lie, you know."

"You put me on the spot!" Baby protested as they rode down the narrow trail. The branches of trees hung low over the path, and it was darker here, without the sun. It was hard to believe they'd been by the ocean just a minute ago. "Since you're apparently the expert, let's hear it."

"Okay. I sing seventies songs before I go onstage for luck, I love porcupines, and I sometimes let pretty girls beat me in a horse race," Riley said.

He was up a little bit ahead of her, and Baby couldn't see his face.

"I bet you *do* sing seventies songs," Baby teased, stalling for time. Had Riley just called her pretty? Her heart was pounding wildly in her chest, and not because Birdie had picked up the pace.

Suddenly, they came to a clearing. "Oh!" Baby exclaimed. They'd reached a small promontory that overlooked the ocean. They really had come to the opposite side of the island, facing a completely different direction than they had before. It was the same ocean, and yet it was even more gorgeous than before. As Baby took in the view, everything felt a million miles away— Manhattan, Constance Billard, even Avery and Owen and her mom and Remington . . .

And Riley's girlfriend?

"I do sing a lot of seventies stuff. It just felt more real back then, you know? All about the music," Riley began as he drew up beside her on the promontory, bringing his horse to a stop. "So that's one." He held up a hand and counted off his answers. "Two, I do love porcupines. They're so weird and so awesome!" He grinned.

Baby sucked in her breath as she waited for him to get to the only answer that mattered to her. She knew he was teasing her, drawing it out. But she couldn't deny that she was enjoying it.

"This view is better experienced on solid ground," Riley announced, easing down off his horse.

"Here," he said, giving her a hand and helping her down off hers. Baby threw her leg over, so that she was perched precariously on the edge of the saddle, facing Riley. She slid down, intending to ease slowly onto the ground. But Birdie had other ideas. The horse jerked forward, throwing Baby off and into Riley's arms.

They stood there for a moment, his dark eyes locked on hers. "And three?" Baby asked, leadingly.

There was a slight curl to his smile, like he knew a secret that he was about to share. "Three . . ." he began, tilting his head ever so slightly toward her. Baby leaned in a little bit closer. She closed her eyes, waiting for his lips to touch hers. . . .

"Hey guys, remember me?"

Baby's eyes wrenched open. She looked up to see Layla approaching, a little ways down the path.

"Oh my God, you guys were so far ahead, I wasn't even sure where you'd gone, but then I remembered how Riley loves this little path," Layla said as she drew nearer. Baby slowly exhaled as she realized that Layla hadn't seen a thing. Riley took a step away from Baby, toward his own horse. "Dusty was, like, about to die," Layla said, panting and out of breath. Her pony looked like it was going to keel over at any moment.

"Sorry—it was just such a nice night for a ride. I got a little carried away," Riley said, pretending to be very interested in one of his stirrups.

"No worries, I know I was going at a glacial pace." Layla shook her head. "Anyway, I'm over this," she said, gesturing to her fatigued pony. "Baby, wanna head back to the villa and get dinner? Riley can commune with his horse or whatever."

Baby glanced over at Riley. She didn't want to leave him. But she knew she should.

"Sure, you girls go ahead," he said. He was staring straight out toward the ocean, his face inscrutable. "I'll catch up with you later."

"Let's see which of our horses can go slower, because I bet mine will win!" Layla joked to Baby, already heading back down the trail. Baby joined her reluctantly, leaving Riley alone.

Never the ideal situation for a Player.

gossipgirl.net

hey people!

Perhaps because it helps us organize our universe, we all have the urge to classify guys into species. Especially on vacation, you notice that there are so many variations and breeds. Each type has its own advantages and drawbacks, and navigating the differences can be tricky. So consider this your very own Gossip Girl Field Guide to Guys.

First—appropriately—there are the alpha males, aka **the Captains of the Team**. They're incredibly gorgeous and studly, and the second they take their shirts off, concentrating on anything else is not an option. But all that testosterone means they're not so in touch with their emotions. Interact with caution: One risks going insane with jealousy while with them because they're such girl magnets.

Then there are the romantics, the guys we call "sweetheart," aka **the Good-Smelling Guys Who Wear Button-Downs**. We can hang out with them all day, like girlfriends, but they're never going to slam us against the wall and tell us, urgently, that they want to see us naked. They're stand-up guys, and they're solid and dependable. But when with them, listen to your own inner yawn alert, because boredom can be a killer.

And then there is the tortured artist, aka **the Guy in the Band**— our hearts melt when he sings to us, but sometimes the beads and scruff and sandals and tattoos can be a little too premeditated and annoying. There's also the potential wild streak: We love a sense of danger and excitement, but someone's bound to get hurt. Proceed with care.

Of course, some guys defy type. And above all, like a good shoe, fit is more important than style. You can pick and choose all you want, but you have to find the guy that's just plain right.

sightings

J's minions **G** and **J** with a group of Scottish twentysomethings at Marquee and Bungalow 8. When the city empties out, you've got to be creative in finding party buddies! . . . **J** by herself in the dressing room of **La Petite Coquette** in the Village, surrounded by heaps of discarded lingerie, eventually just pulling out the black AmEx and buying it all. And that's all the news from my sources on our favorite island. Any news from the *other* islanders? E-mail me! My iPhone works even in this far-flung destination (that I'm still not revealing).

your e-mail

 Dear Gossip Girl,
I think Thanksgiving is just a barbaric, absurd holiday where you have to eat crappy food surrounded by people who don't even like each other. It's like, each year, my parents make me come with them to visit my Grandma Ethel in Greenwich when all she does is hate on me. Is there any way to, like, heal the intergenerational gap?
—SAD

a: Dear SAD,

Vodka gimlets are usually helpful for smoothing the generation gap. If that doesn't work, try taking out her old photo albums, and turn the tables by asking *her* questions about her shady past.
—GG

giving thanks

No matter who you are or where you're celebrating, Thanksgiving is one day to just appreciate the little things and let it all hang out. Wear that comfy magenta Juicy tracksuit that everyone is guaranteed to make fun of but that you love. Enjoy the Muppet movie marathon with your little brother. Eat the pumpkin-gorgonzola-and-bacon risotto your cook made and forget your commitment to vegetarianism, not to mention your diet. Just have fun today, and be thankful that no matter how much you embarrass yourself, no one will know—because I'm taking the day off.

You know you love me,

o hits it up in the hot tub

Rhys quietly closed the door to the bathroom on Thursday morning, hoping he wouldn't wake up the other guys. It was early, but he'd barely slept all night. The villa hadn't exactly been quiet last night. Owen half-talked in his sleep, sounding a bit like he was picking up girls. Even worse, Riley hummed in his sleep. At one point, Rhys had thrown a pillow at him, causing Riley to break out into "More Than a Feelin'."

The question is, *who* does he have more than a feeling for?

Rhys had already taken a shower, shaved, and changed into a pair of khaki shorts and a white linen shirt. He didn't want to look like he was trying too hard, but he also didn't want to look like crap.

"Dude, where are you going?" Owen groaned, rolling over on the bed in the corner.

"Couldn't sleep. Getting food," Rhys whispered.

"Can I come?" Owen asked, already standing on the cool slate slabs of the floor. He was wearing a pair of boxers with little sailboats printed on them.

"Sure." Rhys shrugged. In truth, he sort of wanted to slink

by the girls' villa in case Avery was awake too. They'd sat on the beach yesterday until the sun had set. Avery had talked most of the time, telling Rhys about how she'd always wanted to live in New York City and that now that she *did*, it was so different from what she'd imagined. She'd talked about how her grandmother had been named to *Vogue*'s best-dressed list every year in the sixties, how she'd always had a fabulous winter ball in her town house, how she'd given her jewels from her ex-husbands to her staff since she thought it was bad luck to keep them. Or something like that. Rhys hadn't taken notes or anything, but he'd loved how Avery's blue eyes lit up, how she talked with her hands, how she wasn't afraid to show her enthusiasm.

Finally, they'd gone to meet everyone for dinner at the restaurant in the main hotel, where they'd sat on opposite ends of the table, occasionally catching each other's eye through the flickering candles. Everyone had gone back to the villas and had swum in the pool, but he hadn't had a chance to talk to her alone again, because Owen was there.

"Wanna grab some food by the pool? I bet there's already a lot of girls there. They always get there early to put out their towels and stuff," Owen said knowledgeably as he picked up his gray Nantucket Beach Squad T-shirt from yesterday and pulled it over his head. Rhys wrinkled his nose. He couldn't understand how *anyone* could wear the same clothes two days in a row.

"Sure, pool's fine." Rhys shrugged as he slid open the sliding door. Together, the two guys walked out into the bright sunlight.

"I'm actually glad that we left before Riley got up," Owen confessed as he began walking down the shell-encrusted path that led to the resort proper. "Something about him just seems weird. Do you think he was being flirty last night?" Owen asked.

"Well, you *are* irresistible," Rhys cracked as he pushed his Ray-Bans down over his eyes. Ahead of them was the sprawling, two-story hotel, which looked like it was almost sitting on the blue water. He was *so* glad he was here instead of WestSea Manor, his uncle's drafty country cottage that sat by itself on the middle of a hill in Dorset.

"Asshole." Owen punched Rhys good-naturedly in the arm. "I meant Riley seemed flirty with *Baby*."

They walked inside the palatial lobby, which was decorated in woods and steels. Teak ceiling fans circulated the muggy air. The concierge nodded to both of them as they made their way through the center of the lobby and toward the pool.

"He seems fine, dude. You're on *vacation*. Baby can handle herself," Rhys reasoned. Baby and Riley *had* seemed friendly last night, but the real problem was Owen. It must have been hard to suddenly be expected to bond with his mom's boyfriend, not to mention her boyfriend's daughter and *her* boyfriend. But Owen had such a chip on his shoulder when it came to Remington that he was biased against the whole group—he'd barely spoken two words to Layla, and now he seemed to be obsessing over Riley. Rhys didn't know how to tell his buddy to just chill out. Maybe Owen *did* need to find a girl here, to take his mind off the whole family situation.

They walked onto the patio surrounding the expansive, amoeba-shaped pool. Scattered around were green-and-white striped cabanas, as well as blue lounge chairs.

"Here good?" Rhys asked, gesturing to a cabana by the far edge of the pool.

"Sure." Owen pulled off his shirt and threw it in a messy heap on one of the bamboo chairs. Rhys surveyed the area. The pool was empty, except for a toddler curiously examining a turtle fountain by the edge while his mom watched. It *was* only 10 a.m. on Thanksgiving morning.

"Sirs, can I help you?" a waiter asked. Even the waitstaff's white linen shirts reflected the resort's laid-back but still posh atmosphere.

"I'll have a mimosa," Rhys said. "He'll have one too," he added, ignoring Owen's snort. "You need to lighten up," he said when the waiter walked away.

"Mimosa?! You are such a chick," Owen laughed. "Speaking of chicks, we need to get started on our little mission. So, what do you look for in a girl?"

Rhys shook his head, annoyed that Owen was insisting on going forward with this whole plan. It was enough he was getting hourly texts from Hugh asking about his progress. "Well, I think you know what I like in a girl," he said pointedly. Instantly, the tips of Owen's ears reddened. Good. That oughta shut him up.

"Sorry, man." Rhys shrugged. "Is this the age-old ass-or-chest question again?" The swim team discussed it at least once a week. The team was pretty evenly divided, with Chadwick Jenkins stating that he couldn't decide. As if the skinny, terrified ninth grader actually had girls falling all over him.

"No. I mean, I like girls who know what they want and aren't afraid to go after it," Owen said, furrowing his brow as if he were really thinking it through. The waiter came back with two mimosas garnished with strawberries. Owen chuckled at the berry and drank half the glass in one gulp. He was more of a beer guy.

Rhys racked his brain. What *did* he look for? He'd loved Kelsey's hair, her eyes, her slightly crooked incisor, and her artsy sense of style. Then there had been her enthusiasm and her coral pink lip gloss. . . . It was weird, but the harder he thought about it, the *less* he remembered. They'd dated for so many years, and known each other for so long, that it was hard to remember what exactly had attracted him to her in the first place.

Meanwhile, he knew precisely what he liked about Avery. He loved her silky blond hair, the way he could tell she'd really spent time on her outfits, certain that everything was wrinkle-free and matching, the way she seemed so self-assured—it was even cute when she bossed Owen and Baby around, because at the end of the day it was out of love. And yet, despite her in-charge attitude, Avery seemed a little vulnerable. She was wistful for the glamour of another time. She was, in the truest sense of the word, a romantic.

"Fantasizing?" Owen's sarcastic voice pulled Rhys out of his reverie.

"Only about you," he teased. In truth, the more he thought about Avery, the more he knew he *had* to see her. Even if she *was* Owen's sister, even if he'd promised himself that for now they'd just be friends. She hadn't said what she was doing today, and he wanted to catch her before she went horseback riding or deep-sea fishing or any of the other "family fun" activities Remington had suggested last night at dinner.

"Ha ha." Owen surveyed his friend. Rhys was gazing into his mimosa glass as if it held the secret to the universe.

"I'm going to go," Rhys said suddenly, bolting up off his lounge chair. "Catch you later." He half-jogged off.

"Hey, what about meeting girls?" Owen called to Rhys's retreating back. What the fuck? He picked up Rhys's unfinished mimosa and drained it. Maybe he really *wasn't* over the Kelsey breakup, and talking about other girls made him jumpy. But if so, wasn't the best way for him to get over it to find another girl?

Short answer: Yes. But maybe not the girl he thinks.

Owen leaned back, enjoying the sun on his face. Already, he wanted to go back to sleep. Why had they gotten up so early? And on Thanksgiving, no less. They had plans for a big family dinner, but nothing scheduled for the day. Maybe he could just sleep until dinnertime, right here—

"'Ello, luv! You awake?"

Owen opened one eye. A girl was leaning over him, her tiny, rainbow-colored bikini top just inches from his eyes. Was he dreaming? It was possible he was. Her voice sounded just like the girl's in *My Fair Lady*, Avery's favorite movie when she was little. "Oi! Anything in there?" She tapped a long, acrylic fingernail against Owen's head.

"Sorry, er, hi." Owen pushed himself into a sitting position, blinking his eyes open. The girl had sort of crooked front teeth and short brown hair. Her skimpy bikini showed off her tanned body. Owen sat up straighter.

"Would you mind if I sat 'ere with you? Me mate's 'avin' a lie-in this morning. She had a busy night. 'Onestly, I think everyone round 'ere is mingin'. I'd much rather be in Ibiza, like last year. Instead, I'm here with me mum, so who'm I to say anything? Except that she's bleedin' tedious." The girl pouted as she perched her bony ass on the edge of Owen's chair.

"Uh, yeah," Owen said dumbly. He had no idea what the hell she'd just said. "I can understand about the family stuff, though." He shrugged. It was true.

"I'm Elsie." She extended a hand toward Owen. Owen took it and shook it awkwardly, noticing as he did that her rainbow-colored bathing suit had shifted, exposing part of her boob. For being skinny, she certainly had a huge chest.

So does this mean he's not an ass man?

"Owen. I'm from New York." He tore his eyes away from her chest and focused them on her brown eyes. They were the same color as Chance's, his dog in Nantucket, who they'd left with neighbors when they moved. She was kind of pretty and looked like she was Owen's age, or even a year younger. Maybe he couldn't understand half the words out of her mouth, and maybe she seemed like she'd already had a mimosa or two today. But he was on vacation. Why *not* hang out with her?

Because of the language barrier?

"D'you fancy going into the hot tub?" Elsie asked as she accidentally-on-purpose let the strap of her bikini top fall halfway down her shoulder. She had glittery eye makeup all around her eyes, as if she hadn't bothered to wash her face the night before.

Elsie was smiling devilishly at him. Owen smiled back. He'd always known girls found him attractive, but usually they were much more discreet and just flicked their hair and played with the straps on their tank tops when they talked to him. This was almost *too* easy. "Sure."

Owen took off his shirt and stood. Already, Elsie had scampered over to the oval hot tub that overlooked the ocean.

"So, I have this buddy, Rhys," Owen said as he slid onto the bench of the hot tub. "He's from New York too, and I know he wants to meet new people. You mentioned your friend, who was sleeping in. Is she—"

"Oh my God, Issy's a right tart. It's brilliant! They'll love each other. And then we can also do . . . whatever you'd fancy." Elsie grinned mischievously.

Owen wasn't totally sure what Elsie was saying, but it sounded suspiciously like she was already whoring out her bestie to Rhys. A little more forward than he was used to, but wasn't that the vacation spirit? He looked down and saw a rainbow-colored piece of fabric floating in the hot water. Elsie grinned at him, like they were sharing a secret. Had she just taken her *bathing suit* off? This was the Caribbean, not Europe—was that even allowed?

Somehow, I don't think she's the type to be concerned.

"Well, then, should we get it done and dusted tonight, then?" she asked, arching an eyebrow.

"I can't tonight," Owen said, remembering their family dinner. "But tomorrow for sure."

"Brilliant!" Elsie leaned back, her possibly naked chest and who knew what else concealed underwater. "Tomorrow, then."

Tomorrow, tomorrow—it's only a day away!

love game

"Do you think it's weird that I've never really had a boyfriend?" Avery asked, her eyes flicking away from her *W* magazine.

Baby and Avery had spent the morning on the beach, where Baby was reading the *Bitch* magazine she'd bought and trying not to think about Riley. She hadn't been able to sleep last night and had stayed up staring at the ceiling, replaying their almost-kiss in her head. It was sheer torture knowing he was sleeping in the villa right next door, but that she couldn't go to him—not now, or ever. *It's not right,* she told herself now, as she had a million times over the course of the last twenty-four hours. Layla seemed like a nice person. She liked Layla. So she was going to just forget about Riley, as hard as that seemed at this very moment. The one thing that made it all easier was knowing that after Sunday, she'd probably never see him again.

"Okay, random." Baby perched her vintage Marimekko-style sunglasses on top of her head and closed her magazine. Normally, she couldn't stand lying on the beach doing nothing. She wanted to run, to jump, to explore. But after her sleepless night, it felt good to just do nothing. "No, I don't think it's weird. It only adds to your mystique," Baby decided.

"I don't *want* mystique." Avery shifted on the chair so the sun was falling on her totally flat stomach. She frowned down and squeezed a minuscule amount of skin. "Do you think I'm fat?"

"Okay, you've been hanging out with Jack for *way* too long." Baby rolled her eyes. Of course Avery wasn't fat. She was tall and she wasn't stick-thin, but she always fit into a size two or four.

Which, compared to Baby's size zero, could make any girl feel fat.

"No, it's just I don't understand. . . ." Avery sighed in frustration as she let the sentence trail off. Why hadn't Rhys *done* anything yesterday? Last night after dinner, they'd all gone for a swim. She'd been wearing her orange Eres bikini and had practically been sticking out her chest in front of him, a *very* un-Avery-like move, and still, nothing. Was he not attracted to her? Was their flirtation all in her head?

All of a sudden, she didn't want to talk about it with Baby. She wouldn't understand. Guys fell all over her all the time, even when she hadn't brushed her hair or changed her clothes or washed her face. Right now, she was wearing a blue halter bikini top and baggy Brooklyn Industries shorts and still, three guys running past had given her the once-over. It was so unfair.

"Aren't we supposed to have Thanksgiving dinner early, at like four?" Baby grabbed her margarita and took a long gulp. "We should probably get up there."

"Fine," Avery sighed. Lying here wasn't going to help her make any headway with Rhys, anyway.

Together, they hiked up the limestone steps toward the private pavilion that held the pool and hot tub. Each of the villas had access to the pavilion from their sitting rooms, and from inside the villa you could see the pool. The girls quickly showered and changed, then made their way to meet their family. They were having dinner on the deck of Edie and Remington's villa, served by waiters from the restaurant.

"You're here!" Edie crowed as the girls approached. She was wearing a green-and-blue dress that looked like a toga, a purple orchid haphazardly tucked into her blond bob. "Happy Thanksgiving, my darlings!" Edie swooped down and kissed Avery and Baby on their heads.

She sat back down at the head of the table, which was piled high with bowls of coconuts, pineapple, and mango. It was festive, if it didn't exactly conjure up images of pilgrims and a harvest meal. "We were just playing a getting-to-know-you game!" Edie announced, squeezing Remington's hand.

Fun!

Avery settled into the empty seat beside her mother, with Baby on her other side. Rhys was at the opposite end of the table, next to Owen. He was adjusting his napkin and she wasn't able to catch his eye.

"So, what we do is we go around the table, say our name, and then use an adjective that describes how we're feeling that begins with the letter of our name. So, I'm Edie and I'm *ecstatic* to be here with Remy!" At this, Edie turned and kissed Remington on the lips.

Avery tried not to stare at her mom and Remington kissing—she was sure it was like an eclipse and that too much direct eye contact would make her go blind. She realized it was her turn now. "Um." She glanced around the table, cutting her eyes away when she reached Rhys. "I'm Avery and I'm . . ."

A little bit in love with my brother's best friend?

"I'm always up for an *adventure*," she finished lamely. It was so typical of Edie to make them play a dippy game. Back in Nantucket, they used to always play charades when guests came over. At least she hadn't said anything too embarrassing in front of Rhys.

Everyone looked to Baby next. She could feel Riley's eyes boring holes into her face. He was seated across the table from her, next to Layla, but their seats were a foot apart, and no part of them was touching. "Okay," Baby started, looking down at her plate to avoid Riley's intense gaze. "I'm Baby and I'm—"

"Badass!" Layla exclaimed, reaching across the table and giving her a high five.

"I'll second that!" Riley exclaimed. "You should have seen her on her horse yesterday!"

Baby grinned across the table. Layla seemed so fun and cool, and the more she got to know her, the worse she felt. She caught Riley's eye across the table, and then looked quickly away.

"Okay, Riley, it's your turn!" Edie announced merrily. Two servers came by and set platters of jumbo shrimp on the center of the table. Avery was grateful that her mom didn't ask the servers to participate in their getting-to-know-you game.

"Okay. I'm Riley and I'm *really* looking forward to *riding* again."

Baby looked down at the pink shrimp, knowing he was trying to make eye contact. She hoped she wasn't blushing. Why did he have to bring up their ride?

"Oh, a *double* R! Aren't you a smart cookie!" Edie trilled, already on her third drink. She looked like she wanted to ruffle Riley's hair, but luckily he was too far down the table.

"Yes, I heard you were quite the trailblazer yesterday, Baby," Remington said jovially, helping himself to more shrimp. "I didn't know you rode. You should go again tomorrow. Won't have many chances to ride again once you're back in Manhattan," he added with a wink.

"Oh, I don't—" Baby started, but Riley cut her off.

"I'll take you," he offered, his eyes dancing. "There's a whole other set of trails on the other side of the island we could check out."

"Count me out!" Layla laughed, even though she hadn't been invited. She drained her glass. "That pony made me carsick yesterday. You couldn't pay me to get back on one. Plus, Dad, I want to go out on the boat with you."

"It's settled, then," Riley said, nodding. "Baby and I will go tomorrow."

Baby nodded, not wanting to make a scene. She'd deal with this tomorrow. After all, they were only here for the weekend. How hard could it be to avoid Riley for three more days?

"Okay." Remington cleared his throat as the servers set down tuna tartare, conch mini tacos, and crab rolls on the table. "I'm Remington and I'm *really* in love with Edie."

"Aw, well that makes me even more *ecstatic*!" Edie cooed, a salmon roll halfway to her mouth. Owen set down the lemonade pitcher with such force that the liquid overflowed on the table.

"Nice work," Avery murmured, passing him her napkin. Owen didn't even try to clean up the spill, though. His jaw was set and he was glaring at Remington.

"Listen up, kids," Remington said as he put a hand up, oblivious to Owen's gaze. Even the servers paused to listen. "Being here with all of you—well, it feels like a family." He stood and raised his glass, glancing from face to face. His eyes were actually tearing up. "And I know—I am more sure than I've ever been—that this is what I want for the rest of my life." He turned to Edie as everyone stared in confusion, trying to figure out what was going on. "Edie? Will you marry me?"

Remington knelt down and pulled out a black box from his pocket, flipping it open. A five-carat diamond ring sparkled from inside the box. "Now, I know how you feel about diamonds, but this is an ethical diamond—I checked," Remington babbled, still on one knee.

"What?" Edie said, her mouth full. She stared down at Remington, in shock. "Of course!" she breathed, blinking her enormous eyes. "Of course we'll get married! Does it even need to be a question?" She hugged Remington and beckoned toward the triplets. Remington looked like he was going to faint.

"Oh my God, congratulations!" Avery cried, jumping up and hugging her mother. Sure, it was a little fast, but love was love. And if romance was in the air, maybe Rhys would get a whiff of it.

Is monogamy now airborne?

"You're getting married?" Owen croaked. All the color had drained from his face, and he looked like he was about to throw up.

"Yes, dear," Edie said matter-of-factly, settling back into her chair as if this were the most ordinary of dinners. "Now, let's go on with our game," she said, a bemused expression on her face. "Rhys, it's your turn!"

"Hear! Hear!" Rhys loudly clinked his fork against his Baccarat glass. Riley followed suit.

Baby hollowly began clapping. Her mom and Remington were getting *married*? So much for never seeing these people again. Remington was going to be her stepfather. Layla was going to be her stepsister. And with her luck, she'd probably be the bridesmaid at Layla and Riley's wedding.

Better than the flower girl.

bedroom stories

Jack strode across the marble lobby of the Cashman Lofts and stepped into the private elevator to the penthouse on Thursday evening, a woman on a mission. She hoped J.P.'s family was done with dinner, so she and J.P. could go upstairs and do it already.

Happy Thanksgiving!

She glanced at herself in the gilt gold mirror in the elevator and smoothed her hair. She tried not to be annoyed that all her careful planning had been foiled. Originally, she'd thought they'd get together tonight at her place, where she had everything set up to her precise specifications: Tocca candles at her bedside, a bouquet of freesias sitting on her rolltop desk, and a bottle of Möet in the Sub-Zero downstairs that they could sneak down and have afterwards. But then when her dad had unexpectedly announced this morning that the family was going to come back to the city after their Thanksgiving meal instead of staying overnight in the suburbs, she'd had to hastily rearrange plans.

Jack stepped off the elevator and rang the doorbell, hoping that J.P. would answer, instead of his flashy, former supermodel mom or overly friendly dad.

"Hey beautiful." The door swung open, and revealed J.P. He was wearing a dark blue sweater and khakis. Just like always. "Perfect timing. My parents practically fell asleep at the dinner table," he said, closing the door behind her.

"Good." Jack followed J.P. through the labyrinthine hallways she knew so well and toward the stairs that led to his mini bachelor pad. It was a living area, bedroom, and bathroom that looked remarkably normal, all decorated with sleek black and gray Eames furniture, rather than the mishmash collection of antiques and ultra-modern pieces that populated the rest of the house.

"I'm so glad you came over." J.P. closed the door, twisting its brass lock just to be safe. He dimmed the lights and pressed play on his Bose sound dock. The sound of Coldplay filled the room and Jack tried not to wince. Were they really going to do it to a crappy band that thirty-year-olds listened to?

Well, if it works for Gwyneth . . .

She blocked out the whiny sounds of Coldplay and the thoroughly unromantic track lighting. Who needed champagne and roses and all those other cheesy things? All she needed was J.P. Her boyfriend. Who was perfect.

There's that word again. . . .

"I'm glad we waited," J.P. murmured into Jack's auburn hair as he led her over to his California king horsehair-filled bed.

"Me too," Jack breathed, even though she couldn't help but feel a tugging suspicion that they sounded like characters in a very lame teen movie.

Jack sprawled out on J.P.'s bed, enjoying his gaze. She was wearing a demure silk DVF dress, her black lace La Perla boy shorts and bra underneath. It was underwear she'd worn before, and

J.P. had probably seen it. All of the new bras, corsets, and garters she'd bought from La Petite Coquette were sitting untouched in her bedroom. In the end, it was probably better if she didn't treat it like *such* a big deal. It was just J.P. They'd been together forever. It was more remarkable that they *hadn't* done it, right?

"I love you so much. Always," J.P. whispered earnestly as he stroked her bare arm.

"Kiss me!" Jack replied impatiently. Maybe it'd be better if he just didn't talk. J.P. leaned in and put his lips on hers, his mouth tasting like eucalyptus. His slim fingers played at her back, where her dress was buttoned with tiny mother-of-pearl buttons. He fumbled slightly.

"I'll do it." Jack reached around and undid the buttons, then rearranged herself on the bed, crossing her legs seductively at her ankles.

Just then, her cell beeped from her voluminous blue Balenciaga city bag.

Saved by the bell?

"Should you . . . ?" J.P.'s eyes darted to the corner of the room, where her bag sat.

"Ignore it," Jack commanded. It was kind of fun playing the femme fatale and bossing him around. J.P. kneeled over her, undoing the buttons of his blue-and-white-striped Hugo Boss button-down. He leaned down again and kissed her.

"Harder!" Jack demanded. Usually, J.P. was so sweet and careful when they hooked up, as if afraid she'd break if he wrapped his arms around her too tightly. But now she wanted to feel how much he wanted her.

J.P. leaned toward her chest and kissed upward on her neck. She felt teeth against her skin. Was he *biting* her?

"Actually, not that hard," Jack snapped.

"Sorry!" J.P. said breathlessly, quickly lifting his head up from Jack's collarbone. The top of his head banged hard against her chin.

"Ow!" Jack exclaimed, tears pricking her eyes.

"Oh my God, are you okay?"

"Yeah." Jack rubbed her smooth skin. It would probably bruise. "It's okay," Jack said, wishing J.P. would stop looking at her worriedly and get back to deflowering her. Injuries were *so* not sexy.

Just then her phone chimed again, ringing incessantly. Who on earth was calling her on Thanksgiving?

J.P. sat back on his heels, and Jack sighed, the moment clearly over.

"Are you okay?" J.P. asked, his brown eyebrows knit in concern.

Jack nodded. She was. She knew she could grab him and they could start making out again, ignoring her phone and doing exactly what they'd planned on doing. But all of a sudden, she didn't really want J.P. to touch her. She felt a gnawing hunger in her stomach from skipping dinner, and she really just wanted to watch crappy TV and eat fattening desserts. "Maybe we should do this later," Jack said wearily. She swung her bare feet around the bed and stood on the ugly gold-and-maroon Oriental rug. She hugged her arms to her chest, suddenly self-conscious even though J.P. had seen her in her underwear hundreds of times.

"Of course." J.P. cast his eyes downward as he shuffled toward the bathroom. Jack sighed and picked up her dress from its puddle on the floor. She hated to admit it, but a tiny part of her felt . . . *relieved* at the interruption.

Jack stood and made her way across the room. She rifled through her bag and pulled out her phone.

OMG, my mom just got ENGAGED. It's crazy but I'm happy for them. So much to report, talk soon. Wish you were here! Xo, Ave.

Jack smiled, thinking of her friend. She could tell how excited Avery was just from the text. She pictured Avery, and then Owen, in the middle of an island paradise, celebrating their crazy mother's crazy engagement, raising champagne glasses in the air and having the kind of amazing, life-altering evening she'd hoped to have tonight.

Suddenly, she wished she were there too.

gossipgirl.net

Disclaimer: All the real names of places, people, and events have been altered or abbreviated to protect the innocent. Namely, me.

| topics | sightings | your e-mail | post a question |

hey people!

young and in (long-term) love

So you've met that perfect guy or gal, and you've settled down. Long-term relationships can be great—hello, cozy dinners in, Tuesday-night snuggle sessions, and not having to wear makeup all the time!—and they can make you feel super grown-up. But getting too serious too soon can ruin a relationship. Cases in point: Reese and Ryan. Britney and Kevin. Nick and Jessica. First came love, then came marriage, and in some cases, a baby in a baby carriage. And after that? Divorce.

Of course, not every serious relationship dies a slow death. And I'm not advocating we all stay single forever. But why push a relationship to a place it's not ready to go? Playing the field is so much *fun*, especially while we're young. Don't you want to get out there, meet new people, and *then* see if you're still meant to be? I'm just saying, if it ain't broke, don't put a promise ring on it!

sightings

J in her father's town car, being whisked to JFK. Headed to Paris to visit Maman, or has someone decided to take an impromptu trip? . . . **J.P.**, walking his three puggles in the park, solo. Did somebody get left behind? . . . **S.J.**, **J**, and **G**, coming out of hot spot 1Oak in the wee hours. Doesn't anybody stay in on Thanksgiving anymore? . . . Lastly, swim team playboy **H**, cozily ensconced in a booth at **Rose Bar** with a very flirty French girl giving him some very flirty French kisses. Hope she didn't notice him texting under the table! Who could be important enough to divide his attention?

your e-mail

q: Dear Gossip Girl,
So, I met this guy and we had so much fun, and we even made out. He took my number and said he'd call. But then he didn't. It's been a week and I haven't heard from him, and I've hung around the spot where we met but still no sign of him. What gives?
—hoodiegirl

a: Dear H,
I'll keep it short, but not so sweet: Sounds like he's just not that into you. Sorry!
—GG

the parent trap

Finally, it's come to my attention that some people are missing their basic manners when it comes to behaving themselves appropriately while being hosted by another family. Yes, it can be weird to hang out with parents who aren't your own. But think of it this way: If they decide you're a good influence on their offspring, you'll be showered with college recommendations and cool presents and receive a carte blanche invite to their house. So keep your eye on the prize and follow these three ultra-simple rules.

Flatter the mom. Ask her who her stylist is. Tell her how young/tiny/amazing she looks, even if she's obviously squeezing into a way-too-small size four and has highlights circa Memorial Day.

Don't get drunk at dinner. There are plenty of opportunities to do that sans the parents, so don't just chug their vintage 1980 L'Evangeline bordeaux. Especially since you probably participated in drinking that other bottle they think they misplaced.

Stay out of their way! Remember, most parents don't *really* want to do the intergenerational bonding thing—they just want to make sure their children act suitably appropriate and are entertained. Prove that you're entertaining and appropriate, and they'll be more than happy to keep their distance.

And, for extra credit—or if you're trying to score that seventeenth-birthday Mercedes—try using these rules on your *own* parents. After all, your own parents deserve the same kind of respect that you show to Muffy and Jim from the club, don't they?

As if it weren't easy enough already.

You know you love me,

pooling resources

Rhys tossed and turned on the yellow Egyptian cotton sheets as the sky outside the window changed from gray to gold; the sun was just beginning to rise. He was tired, but for the second night in a row, he couldn't sleep. Maybe it was the heat.

Or maybe it was the fact that Avery was probably only sleeping five feet away, separated by the thin bamboo villa wall.

"Bro, you ready?"

Rhys squinted one eye open at Owen, who was wearing a white T-shirt and cargos. He looked impatient. "I want to leave before Remington knocks on the door and suggests family bonding activities," Owen explained.

"Okay, give me a second." Rhys sighed as he swung his feet onto the cool stone floor. The whole engagement announcement had really messed with Owen's head. He'd been quiet at the dinner last night, just drinking more and more until he pretty much passed out in the villa.

"Don't obsess over your clothes," Owen ordered as he flung open Rhys's closet, surveying his clothing options. "Those British girls I was telling you about are looking forward to meeting you, and they don't give a fuck about what shirt you're wearing. I did the heavy lifting, bro. You can thank me later."

Rhys wished Owen had forgotten about Hugh's dumb challenge. But given Owen's current state of mind, the least Rhys could do was pretend to go along with his plan. "Did your *mom* pack for you?" Owen scoffed as he surveyed the neatly hung button-downs and folded piles of board shorts.

"No," Rhys said shortly as he grabbed a pair of cargos and a blue linen button-down shirt. His mom totally *would* have packed for him if they'd had more time. She had even slipped a cheesy card into his duffel as he was leaving, as if he were a four-year-old heading to his first day of nursery school at All Souls.

Rhys walked into the bathroom and surveyed himself critically in the mirror. *Not bad.* Not bothering to shave, he splashed some Acqua di Parma aftershave lotion onto his face.

"Dude, come on!" Owen knocked on the door impatiently. Rhys suppressed a sigh and mussed his hair up slightly.

He closed the bathroom door and followed Owen out of the villa's sliding glass doors. They walked along the winding path to the main resort. The sun was making its way higher into the sky, casting patterns of light against the sand-covered path. Birds were chirping in the trees as if they were part of an ambient music CD, and a light breeze made the heat feel inviting, rather than intolerable. It would be totally romantic with the right person, Rhys thought, instead of with a moody male buddy. Owen was kicking the seashells in his path almost violently. Rhys knew he was thinking about Remington and his mom.

"Dude, you okay about everything?" Rhys asked. They could see the resort now, the orange-and-cream-colored structure seemingly jutting out toward the ocean.

"I will be. I just need to hook up," Owen repeated. He was starting to sound like a broken record, but Rhys decided that probably wasn't the smartest thing to point out. "And *you* do too."

"I know. Hugh reminds me every fucking hour," Rhys said, annoyed. Didn't Hugh have a family to distract him?

They walked silently over to the large pool area, collecting dark blue embroidered towels from a bored-looking girl at the towel hut.

"There's Elsie. I guess that must be her friend." Owen directed his gaze over to two girls in the pool. One had long, peroxide-blond hair and the other had short curly brown hair. From a distance, it didn't look like either girl was wearing a top.

"Owen!" one called in an accent. "'Ello love. Won't you come 'ere!" Rhys cringed. Was Owen serious about these girls? She sounded *exactly* like his cousin Archie's wife, Nicola. Nicola wore pink Juicy sweat suits and gold hoop earrings and always got drunk on Diet Coke and vodkas at family functions, even though she was technically the Duchess of Kent. It was one of the many scandals in the Sterling family.

And probably not the last.

"And that's your mate, innit? Bring 'im over, let's 'ave a look, now!" the blond girl called shrilly. Rhys wished he could head back to the villa.

"Did I hook us up or *what*?" Owen eagerly peeled off his shirt and waded into the shallow end of the pool as he swum over to the brunette. Rhys paused a moment, then took off his own linen shirt and folded it into a neat pile. Maybe by the time he was done folding it, they'd be gone.

"'Ello!" the blond girl said, wringing out her hair and dripping water all over Rhys's Reef sandals. Her ugly silver-and-gold triangle bikini top barely covered her enormous boobs. She smiled, revealing extremely crooked teeth. Kelsey had had a slightly crooked incisor that middle-school orthodontia hadn't helped, but on her it was adorable. This girl looked like she'd never seen the inside of a dentist's office. "Me mate, Elsie, over there told me she'd met your man yesterday, innit? Glad you're here. I'm Isobel. Well, that's me proper name and all, but me best mates and even me mum all calls me Issy. And who are you?" Issy looked Rhys up and down expectantly.

"Rhys." He stuck out his hand. Issy shook it enthusiastically. She had four-inch bright red acrylic nails. "I guess, then, we might as well go over to your, um, mate?" Rhys asked, wading into the water. He headed toward the swim-up bar on the other end of the pool, where Owen and Elsie were already ordering drinks. He *really* didn't want to be left alone with Issy.

"Hi!" Rhys said abruptly, wedging himself between Owen and Elsie at the submerged bar.

"So, you met Issy, then? I'm Elsie." The girl with the curly brown hair glanced away from Owen. "You look nice."

"Thanks." Issy and Elsie? How was he even going to keep them straight? Rhys turned to the bartender. In order to get through this, he needed a drink. "I'll have a mimosa."

"Can I 'ave one?" Elsie asked, sidling up beside him.

"Uh, sure." Rhys didn't want to be rude.

"Actually, can I have a Sex on the Beach?" Elsie locked eyes with Issy and the two of them began howling with laughter. With the perfect palm trees swaying in the breeze, the crisp morning air and the turquoise water, Rhys felt like he'd been dropped into some bad vacation movie.

Weekend at Elsie's?

"You got it, my man!" The dreadlocked bartender winked at Rhys like they were sharing a joke.

"So, um, where are you from?" Rhys began. He took a large gulp of his mimosa. It was nowhere near as strong as he needed.

"Essex." Elsie—Issy?—said proudly.

Rhys cringed. From what he remembered his cousins telling him, Essex was sort of like the Queens of England. In fact, that was where his cousin's wife Nicola was from. Why were these British girls here over an American holiday weekend, anyway? It was like they'd come here to prey on unsuspecting American boys on *their* vacations, just when they were at their weakest.

Not a bad supposition . . .

"Her mum 'ad an affair with some footballer bloke, but she's well hacked off 'e's always off playin' and never round, so 'e sent 'er on 'oliday until she felt sorted. So Elsie brought me, which is blindin' good! Bunch of duffers here, innit?" Issy asked. She took the pink drink in front of her and easily polished it off.

"Huh?" Owen looked mystified. Rhys cracked a half-smile, feeling like he'd landed on another planet.

"Um, they're on vacation here with Elsie's mom, who's dating a soccer star. I think they're happy that they came together, because most people at the resort are older," Rhys translated, remembering the group of English kids they used to hang out with at a pub in London that Rhys's cousin had loved.

"Rhys is British," Owen announced proudly. Rhys signaled to the bartender for another drink. Whatever Issy was speaking, it wasn't *British*.

And it only gets *easier* to understand with more drinks!

"Oh. And what are *you*?" Elsie licked her bright pink lips lasciviously at Owen.

"Where are you from, then?" Issy asked at the same time, turning so that she was facing Rhys. She put her hand on his knee. Rhys could feel her acrylic nail tips digging into his skin.

He glanced at Owen for a rescue, but Owen and Elsie had swum over to the other end of the bar.

"We're actually from New York City," Rhys said shortly. No way did he want to get into a discussion about his family tree. "How's your drink?"

"All gone!" Issy shook her head sadly as she stared down at her empty glass. "Barman? Can I 'ave another Sex on the Beach?" She played with the green flamingo-shaped stirrer in her drink, biting onto it with her crooked tooth.

"Sure thing!" The dreadlocked bartender nodded.

"'Ave you ever had it?" Issy asked, holding the stirrer in her mouth as if it were some sort of absurd cigarette.

"I like beer better. So, how long are you on vacation for?" Rhys asked politely. If she lost the accent, the attitude, and the gold hoop earrings that were turning her earlobes green, Issy might be pretty. But still, he couldn't help comparing her to Avery. She'd looked beautiful last night, her hair falling softly around her athletic shoulders, her Tiffany silver bracelets shining against her slim, tanned wrists, her blue eyes so wide and sparkly. But it was more than that. It was the way she'd seemed so genuinely enthusiastic about her mom's announcement. Unlike other girls Rhys had known, who were jealous or selfish or only pretended to be happy for other people, Avery genuinely wanted everyone around her to be happy.

"I'm not talking about the drink, mate!" Issy laughed, throwing her head back so her platinum blond hair fanned out in the water behind her. "I mean, 'ave you ever shagged on the beach?"

"No." Rhys's ears turned bright red.

"Oh, sorry, don't be embarrassed!" Issy protested, grabbing Rhys's hand underwater. Her muddy brown eyes looked almost sad.

"Is Rhys not being nice?" Owen asked as he swam up to the two of them, Elsie clinging to the back of his neck. Rhys wasn't sure if he should be happy that his friend was sort of rescuing him or livid that Owen had put him in this situation in the first place.

"I thought you American blokes were supposed to be adventurous. This one seems shy," Issy pouted, as though Rhys wasn't sitting right next to her. He sighed. At least the bartender, probably taking pity on him, had already refilled his drink.

"He's not when you get to know him," Owen said.

"So, where's the wildest place you've shagged?" Issy asked curiously. "I'll go first. In the McDonald's bathroom with me mate, Ben. When we got out, our fries wasn't even cold!" she announced proudly.

"Oi, but then you got an ASBO and couldn't go back there again for a bleedin' six months." Elsie rolled her eyes. "Anti-Social Behavior Order, from the government. She's got loads," she added, noting Owen and Rhys's confused expressions.

"What about you, Rhys?" Issy asked pointedly.

"Um, we don't have Antisocial . . . things in the US," Rhys said.

"I'm not talking about that. I don't know why Elsie brings it up, she knows I'm right hacked off about it," Issy sighed in annoyance. "No, where's the wildest place you've shagged?"

"He's working on it," Owen jumped in.

Thanks. Rhys shot an annoyed look at Owen.

"Does that mean you've never been shagged?" Issy asked in disbelief.

"I . . . I just went through a breakup." Rhys looked toward the ocean, almost wishing he were in *real* England instead of bizarre England with these girls.

"Ohhhh, I can help you! I'd be gentle. I'm very good," Issy added, as if she were on a job interview.

"She really is good. And she ain't fussy when it comes to blokes to get it off with. She's done well worse than you," Elsie added generously, sucking down the rest of her drink.

Rhys could feel the tips of his ears turn pink. Of *course* she'd done *well worse* than him. He was about to say something to this effect when Issy interrupted.

"Oi, all this drinking and now I've gotta pee like a racehorse! Rhys dear, watch me drink for me?" Issy was already climbing out of the pool, her tiny swimsuit giving her a wedgie that she didn't correct. By some unspoken girl code, Elsie was already climbing out of the pool, following her.

Rhys slid off the tiled bench of the bar and swam toward the other side of the pool, not even bothering to check to see if Owen was following behind him. Even though he'd only had a few drinks, his stroke was uneven, and the water felt heavy. He stopped at the other end and held on, looking out onto the blue ocean.

"I did good, huh? They're all over us!" Owen exclaimed, holding his hand up for a high five as he treaded water beside him. He withdrew his hand when Rhys didn't slap it. "Is something wrong?"

Where to even begin?

"I'm just not feeling Issy," Rhys said honestly, gazing out at the ocean. All the way down the beach, he could just make out a couple splashing in the water. At one point, the girl playfully broke into a run, pulling the guy into the water with her. They kissed in the splashing waves like a movie.

"What, are you upset about the virgin thing? She was just teasing. But she seems totally cool about the whole thing. And she's English, too, so you already have something in common." Owen pointed out, looking extremely pleased with himself.

"No, it's not that. I just can't," Rhys said, not sure what to say to get Owen to lay off. Owen's face looked so proud and hopeful, and it was the first time he'd seen a smile on his friend's face since the engagement shocker last night. Besides, he couldn't tell him that the real reason he didn't want to sleep with Issy—or anyone else, for that matter—was that he was possibly in love with his sister.

Rhys reached for a lie instead. "I guess I'm just not over Kelsey," he said, instantly feeling bad as he watched Owen's expression fall.

"Okay, man. I get it," Owen said woodenly. Issy and Elsie had emerged from the bathroom and were waving to them from the other side of the pool.

"I'll hang out for a little bit longer," Rhys offered, feeling guilty.

"Thanks," Owen said, not really listening. As he swam toward Elsie, who was doing a sexy little come-hither dance, the air seemed to escape from his lungs. Earlier he'd been looking forward to a few days of fun, meaningless sex, but suddenly he felt like a giant douche.

Rhys was still hung up on Kelsey, and Owen had thought that he was just as head over heels for her as his buddy had ever been.

And yet, a month later, he barely thought of her. He'd thought he loved Kelsey, but clearly it was just lust.

It is better to have loved and lost than never to have loved at all, Owen thought randomly, recalling the quote from a poetry unit back in his Nantucket English class. Rhys had loved Kelsey. Baby had had a string of boyfriends, each of whom she'd loved in her own way. Layla and Riley had been together for years, which meant they had to love each other. Even his *mom* had found love—not that he was thrilled about her marrying Remington, but still.

Everyone else in his life, for better or for worse, had found someone they clicked with, someone they forged a real, honest connection to, at least once in their life. But apparently, Owen didn't even know what love felt like.

As he swam toward Elsie and her teeny-tiny string bikini, he was starting to doubt that he ever would.

besties on the beach

"Oh my God! Jack!"

Baby woke up to squeals emanating from the sitting room. What the hell? She'd been having this weird dream where she'd been in charge of planning Riley and Layla's wedding, except somehow, she'd ended up marrying both of them. It seemed very weird and Freudian and she was sort of glad to be woken up.

"What are you doing here?!"

Baby hadn't heard Avery so excited since she'd won the Miss Lobster Queen title back in ninth grade. What the hell *was* Jack Laurent doing here? Didn't she have enough lives to ruin in New York? Baby closed her eyes again, hoping it was just some sort of weird dream-within-a-dream.

"Well, I missed you." Jack's voice carried through to the other room.

"I can't believe your dad let you come! This is so perfect!" Avery cried, completely ignoring the fact that Baby and Layla were sleeping in the next room. Or rather, Baby was pretending to sleep. She rubbed the sleep from her eyes and padded over to her suitcase, which was bursting with flowy, cottony dresses, cutoff skirts, and bathing suits. She'd never been a good packer, preferring to just throw the contents of a drawer into her suitcase and see what happened. Besides, she could always borrow from Avery. She rifled through her suitcase until she found a string bikini and a skirt she'd made out of a pair of Avery's discarded Sevens. She pulled on an aquamarine thrift store T-shirt that had a Blue Bunny ice cream logo on the front. She'd cut the back into strips to give it a little bit of punk sex appeal. Avery hated the shirt, which was why she wore it.

She walked across the cool stone floors and opened the door to the sitting room, where Avery was pawing through Jack's Louis Vuitton duffel trunk. The two girls were totally oblivious to her presence.

"Is this new?" Avery demanded, holding up a strappy lemon-colored dress in front of her frame. Jack was wearing a similar dress in apricot. "I like it."

"Of course you do. Did you notice you're wearing the same one?" Baby said, interrupting their fashion show. Was their friendship really just about complimenting each other's clothes all the time?

"Oh, your sister's here." Jack glanced up from her perch on the brown-and-white-striped love seat. "Nice shirt," she said, not even bothering to hide her sarcasm. Ever since J.P. and Baby had briefly dated, Jack had made it no secret that she hated Baby. Now that she and Avery were friends, Jack wasn't overtly mean, but the two of them tried to stay out of each other's way.

"Why are you here?" Baby asked directly.

"I needed a change from New York." Jack shrugged but didn't offer any more details. That was the truth, after all. Jack had left J.P.'s quickly after their non-attempt at sex and had gone back to the town house, where her family had already come back from their dinner at Rebecca's parents'. As soon as she stepped in the door, she knew she had to get out. The twins had been especially loud, hopped up on too much pumpkin pie and Dora the Explorer, and her dad and stepmom had seemed exhausted and harried. Jack saw a future weekend of babysitting flash before her eyes, and she knew she simply couldn't maintain her sanity with the Wiggles as her weekend sound track. She booked a ticket to the Bahamas, explaining to her dad and J.P. that Avery needed her for emotional support. Her dad had consented, probably because he was far too exhausted dealing with the twins to protest, and J.P. had been nice about it, if a little disappointed. He told her to take plenty of pictures and that he would be there in spirit. It was sweet.

Maybe too sweet?

"Baby just wears that to piss me off." Avery stuck her tongue out at her sister.

"You guys are so loud," Baby whined as she walked over to the sliding doors. She flung them open, taking a moment to admire the way the sun reflected on the water. Instantly, she calmed down a little bit. Yeah, Jack Laurent sucked, but at least the scenery was nice.

"So, are you hanging out with Layla today?" Avery called out to Baby.

Baby shrugged. She knew Avery well enough to know that meant that she'd rather Baby not hang around with her and Jack. Not like she'd want to. They'd probably spend the whole day lying on the beach, followed by hours at the spa. Baby was sick of just lying around. She wanted to *do* something.

Or, um, someone?

Baby wandered back into the sitting room. "Oh, I forgot. There's a note for you. I think it's from Remington," Avery said, her arms elbow-high in Jack's suitcase as she examined its contents with the precision of a surgeon.

"Weird," Baby mumbled, wondering why on earth her mom's boyfriend—make that fiancé—was writing her. She picked up the note from the countertop and saw that it was in fact from Remington, letting her know that he had set everything up for her and Riley to go riding today.

"I guess he made us some riding reservations," Baby explained. She glanced from a distracted Avery over to Jack, who seemed impatient to get rid of her. Even though she'd planned on avoiding Riley, hanging out with him suddenly seemed like her best option. "I'd better head down that way." She grabbed a pair of jeans to wear later and headed out the doors and onto the wrap-around patio.

"'Bye," Jack called sweetly. Baby didn't bother to respond.

"Is this good?" Avery called to Jack, choosing a blue-and-white cabana at one end of the hotel pool. Since Jack had arrived an hour ago, Avery had been dying to delve into a long, girly conversation. Baby was her sister and all, but for some reason Avery hadn't wanted to talk to her about the Rhys thing. Besides, she wanted some outsider perspective on her mom's engagement.

"Sure!" Jack sprawled on one of the linen-covered lounge chairs and sighed. "God, this is so much better than New York. It was so boring without you! And the stepbrats were fucking monsters. Remind me to never have children." Jack shuddered and pushed her D&G sunglasses on top of her auburn hair.

"Don't tell me, tell J.P.!" Avery giggled. She pulled her container of Bliss suntan lotion out of her See by Chloé watermelon pink beach bag and slowly squeezed some onto her arms.

"Yeah, that's not going to happen." Jack rolled her eyes. "Can I have some of your sunscreen?" She held out a dainty, manicured hand.

Avery regarded Jack curiously. Even though she and Jack had become good friends in the past month, she'd never really heard Jack talk about anything personal. Instead, they'd talk about sample sales, totally unacceptable behavior by other Constance students, what parties they were going to go to, and what they were going to wear. Thinking about it, Avery didn't know Jack's favorite color or if she'd slept with a stuffed animal when she was little or if she ever had braces or any of the totally normal things you were *supposed* to know about a best friend. It seemed Jack had been born totally beautiful, confident, and sure of herself. Or at least, she wanted everyone to believe that. Avery knew from firsthand experience—when she'd discovered Jack living in the tiny garret above her former town house after her dad cut her and her mom off—that Jack had her own insecurities and hidden secrets.

Avery was about to find the politest way to probe Jack about J.P. when she noticed a group of people on the other side of the pool. Avery could just make out a blond guy and a brown-haired guy, sitting beside two scantily clad girls, drinking and playing in the water. It was Owen.

And *Rhys*.

She couldn't see Rhys's face, since he was turned toward the submerged bar, but she certainly saw one of the girl's arms draped possessively around his neck. They were at least fifty yards away, but Avery thought she could even hear them laughing. There were empty glasses on the edge of the pool on either side of them. And it was what, 11 a.m.? Had they just been there all morning, drinking and flirting? Were they on a *double date*?

"What?" Jack asked curiously. Avery was stuffing her towel and sunblock back into her beach tote. She motioned toward the pool.

"I know when Owen's flirting. I don't want to ruin his game," Avery lied. She ignored the tears pricking her eyes. "Besides, no one's here, anyway. I want to go to the beach."

"Owen?" Jack asked, standing up to follow Avery's gaze. From across the pool, she suddenly saw what Avery was staring at. She recognized Owen's shock of blond hair and his white teeth as he threw his head back, laughing at something Rhys Sterling had said. Or maybe it was something one of those skanky girls with them had said. They were hot in that trashy, look-at-me sort of way, and one of the girls was practically rubbing herself against Owen's tanned torso. Jack suddenly felt like she was going to be sick, and it wasn't from the early morning flight.

She grabbed her things and went to follow Avery toward the beach, glad that they weren't sticking around to watch. She suddenly felt extremely stupid and extremely annoyed with herself. What had she been thinking—that she'd arrive in the Bahamas and fall immediately into Owen's arms?

Avery marched away, her cork Hollywould platforms thwacking down the sandstone stairs. She swiped at her eyes with the back of her hand, hating herself for getting so upset. An uneven black smear of mascara stayed on her hand. Fuck. Why was she wearing mascara to the beach, anyway? To impress Rhys? It was so stupid. It wasn't like they'd even *kissed*. And yet for the first time in her life, she felt like she'd let a guy make a total and complete fool out of her.

The white strip of beach below the pool was set up with the same blue-and-white striped cabanas as the hotel. Avery quickly popped into one. She needed to relax and regroup, and hopefully avoid Rhys and his new girlfriend. At least until she was appropriately rested and fabulous.

"Would you ladies like a drink?" A skinny beach waiter in khaki shorts and a white linen shirt poked his head into the cabana, proffering woven straw menus.

Jack waved the menus away. "Mimosas. And muffins. And French toast," she added. "We're on vacation, fuck calories," Jack announced as she pulled off her flowy white Milly sundress and tossed it onto the sand, revealing her black Calvin Klein halter bathing suit.

Avery shot her a grateful smile, suddenly feeling a teeny bit better. It was really sweet of Jack to sympathy-eat with her, even though Avery hadn't told her what was going on.

"And Danish!" Avery called after the waiter. Why not? She might as well feed her sorrows. She pulled off her own green-and-orange Lilly Pulitzer dress and readjusted the straps of her gold Eres bikini. There. She had her best friend, the sun, and someone catering to her every whim. Forget Rhys. She'd be fine.

"Okay, so details!" Jack pressed after she had settled onto her back. "Your mom's getting married."

"Yeah," Avery said, nodding. *Right*. The engagement. That was why Jack thought she was upset. Which was good, because she really didn't feel like talking about Rhys, now that she knew he'd never even liked her in the first place. "You know, Remington's kind of weird, but my mom loves him. And he loves her." *And he doesn't flirt with half-naked pool sluts,* she thought mutinously.

Jack blinked her green eyes toward Avery, nodding in

understanding. "Well, it's better than my mom. She's having an affair with a fucking nineteen-year-old French dude named Guillaume. I mean, really, what the fuck?" Jack began, even though she didn't really want to talk about her mom and Guillaume. Or about Avery's mom and her weird fiancé. Ever since she saw Owen's white-blond hair and broad shoulders from across the pool, all she wanted to talk about was *Owen*. She couldn't believe she had just left him with those sluts. Jack knew she was being ridiculous—it wasn't like Owen could have known she was coming. But seeing him with someone else had hurt, in a way that seeing J.P. with Baby Carlyle never had.

"Boys are all asses." Avery sighed as the waiter appeared with a carafe of mimosas, along with a tray of French toast and a basket with mixed Danish and muffins.

"Including your brother?" Jack asked, she hoped subtly. She flipped over to her stomach and undid her straps so she wouldn't get any weird tan lines.

"Well, he's always been a player," Avery said as she grabbed a Danish. She bit into it, but it was stale and hard. "At least in Nantucket he was. But since we got to New York, it was pretty much just him and Kelsey. You know, until he pretended to date *you*." Avery shook her head, remembering when Owen and Jack had pretended to be a couple. Avery put the Danish down and plucked a blueberry muffin from the basket. While it had been a bitchy and devious move on Jack's part, it was almost flattering that Jack had gone to such great lengths to get under her skin. "But back in Nantucket, he hooked up with everyone."

"Really?" Jack wrinkled her nose. She sounded a little upset, but Avery couldn't tell behind her enormous D&G sunglasses.

"Why do you want to know?" Avery asked, suddenly suspicious. Did Jack have a crush on Owen or something? But what about her boyfriend?

"Is everything okay with J.P.?" Avery asked point-blank.

"Yeah, everything's fine," Jack said, suddenly very focused on rubbing sunscreen into her tan arms. "The stepbrats' nanny has off until Monday and it's brutal. I needed to get out of the house. And, of course, I wanted to see you!" Jack added.

"Okay," Avery said uncertainly. She closed her eyes and tried to focus on the feeling of the sun baking her skin. But she couldn't relax. The excitement of the morning had dissipated, and in its place she felt only disappointment and exhaustion.

"You know, I'm actually really tired," Avery said, standing up. She felt bad ditching Jack, but right now, she wasn't going to be much fun anyway. "I was up late last night and I think I just need a quick catnap. I'll call the desk to have a key card made for you," Avery said as she slung her bag over her shoulder. "Bye!"

She didn't wait for Jack's response as she walked the long way up the beach, so she wouldn't have to cross the pool. All along the sand were couples of all ages. Everyone looked so *happy*. What was her problem?

Avery hurried toward the villa. Maybe she could just take a nap, and when she woke up this entire morning would be like a dream.

In fairy tales, only Prince Charming can wake you. . . .

the sea is not calm for b

Baby sat hugging her knees to her chest on the teak chair outside the guys' villa. It had been almost an hour since she left Avery and Jack, and she'd intended to knock on the door, grab Riley, and go riding. But as soon as she'd gotten here, she'd hesitated. Layla wasn't in the room when she woke up. What if she was with Riley, like, doing it or something?

"Howdy, partner," Riley said, emerging from the villa. His hair was spiky, as if he'd put product in it, and he was wearing a red flannel shirt cut off at the sleeves, along with jeans. "Have you been waiting out here? Why didn't you just come inside?"

Baby shrugged. "Looks like it's just the two of us. I think Layla and her dad are getting breakfast together," Riley explained. "Ready to ride?"

"If you are." Baby smiled. She and Riley started walking toward the golf carts, and easily fell into step. At only five feet tall, Baby was used to practically having to run to keep up with the strides of guys she dated. But Riley was good about walking in step with her, almost as if he were doing it on purpose.

"Hop in." Riley nodded to the passenger side of the golf cart.

"I'm driving today." Baby arched an eyebrow and slid into the driver's seat.

"You're on. I like a woman who can giddy up and go." Riley smirked as he walked over to the passenger side of the cart.

"So, are you going to tell horse jokes all morning?" Baby asked sarcastically.

"Probably." Riley smiled as Baby turned on the ignition and began driving down the bumpy dirt road that wound around the other private villa compounds. It was pretty here, but almost too perfect. With the bright blue sky, the lush palm trees, and the incessant birdcalls, it felt like she'd stumbled into some dream world.

"So, your mom's getting married. That's pretty wild," Riley said. He drummed his slender fingers against his knees as if accompanying the beat of some song only known to him.

"Remington's a good guy. I just want them to be happy, you know? I mean, we're all going to be out of the house in two years. . . . I just don't want her to be lonely." Baby tore her eyes away from Riley's fingers and concentrated on the road. Why was she spilling to Riley? Next thing she knew, she'd tell him she had a huge crush on him.

"He is a good guy. And it's a little fast, but I guess you know when you know," Riley mused, looking at Baby in that secretive way again. "Like, when—wait, stop here!"

Baby abruptly slammed on the brake.

"We're here." Riley smiled and shook his head. "You love the gas pedal, don't you? I'm going to call you Trigger," he teased as he slid out of the golf cart.

They walked up the grassy hill to the stables. For Baby, it felt natural to be with Riley. *But what about Layla?* she wondered.

"You've got a cool family," Riley said.

"Thanks. What about yours? Are they sad you weren't home for Thanksgiving?"

"Right." Riley gave a short laugh that sounded like a bark. "I'm from Texas. It's big hats, big hair—my dad thinks I'm gay because I like music. He's on his fifth wife. Second runner-up for Miss Texas." Riley shook his head. "It's easier to forget about them and just do what I want."

"I can understand that." Baby nodded. Riley quickened his pace and walked into the door to the stable. "I'll get the horses ready," he called.

Baby settled on a wooden glider swing set up outside the stable and slowly pushed herself back and forth with her foot. She loved Riley's lilting Texas accent and the way he stared in her eyes, as if he really wanted to know what she was thinking. His flirty jokes were actually funny, and it seemed he was telling them as much for his own amusement as hers. He seemed honest. He wasn't trying to make his past seem perfect.

"Here you go," Riley said, carrying a plastic step stool under one arm and leading a large bay with the other. He tenderly patted her nose. "I brought you Boots. She and I've got a history."

"Should I—I mean, Layla, be jealous?" Baby asked as she slid off the glider and walked toward the horse. Oops. She'd almost made it sound like *they* were a couple.

"Nah," Riley said. Something flickered over Riley's face at the mention of Layla's name, but he didn't seem to want to go into it. He put the step stool down on the sandy grass. "Step up."

Baby swung her leg up and over the horse's broad back.

"Whoa!" Baby involuntarily exclaimed. This horse seemed even bigger than the one from a couple of days ago. "You sure she's nice?"

"You can handle her." Riley grinned and picked up the step stool. "I'll be right back."

Quickly, he emerged on his own horse, the same one he'd ridden before Wednesday. He cantered past Baby, and Boots followed his lead.

"Okay. Help me be good, okay, girl?" Baby whispered into the horse's velvety ear. It whinnied, as if to say, *Yeah, right!*

"No fair! You can't tell secrets to the horses. That's one of the rules!" Riley called in front of her as the horses picked their way down the sandy grass and toward the beach. "For that, we're gonna run!" He kicked his horse in the flanks. Boots quickly followed suit, galloping onto the white sand.

"Hey!" Baby yelled, gripping the reins and feeling the wind whip through her hair. She wasn't scared, though. For some strange reason, she trusted Riley. He reminded her of her old self, the free-spirited girl she'd been growing up on Nantucket.

"There's a cove I want you to see. Follow me!"

"Cool," Baby said. The sun had already risen high in the sky and Baby felt sweat begin to bead on her forehead. She'd never thought horseback riding was such a workout, but it really was. She rode in silence for a little while, following Riley's strong, confident form up ahead.

"Here we are!" Riley called as they reached a small inlet, tucked away from the shore. There were no hotels or villas that Baby could see, just an endless expanse of white sand and blue water. It was beautiful.

Boots seemed to think so too. The horse curiously plodded its way toward the water.

"Is she allowed to do that?" Baby called nervously. She didn't want her horse to drown.

Back on shore, Riley swung his cowboy-booted foot off his own horse and led her to a worn wooden post stuck at the point where the beach met grass. He took off his boots, pulled off his jeans, and waded into the ocean in his green plaid boxer shorts. He reached down into the water and flicked some drops up onto Baby, who looked down on him from her horse.

"Hey!" Baby cried as he splashed her.

"What? Boots was giving herself a bath, just thought I'd help out." Riley shrugged mock innocently, his eyes crinkling adorably at the corners. "But I think she's had enough. What do you say we give her a break and cool off ourselves?" Riley grabbed Boots's bridle and walked her up to the hitching post.

As he hitched Boots to the post, Baby looked down at his muscular arms and surprisingly chiseled torso and imagined what it'd be like to have them wrapped around her waist. She realized she was staring and quickly drew her eyes away.

"I just love horses. They're so simple, you know?" Riley said, almost to himself, as he gently stroked Boots's shiny coat.

Baby nodded, thinking of the myriad of animals her family had left behind in Nantucket. She missed her dog Chance, not to mention their cats, fishes, and turtles. Baby had always felt more comfortable with animals. She'd been convinced she could communicate with Chance through blinking, and would sometimes sit with him for hours, staring into his soulful brown eyes. In some ways, she felt like she'd left some of her best friends behind in Nantucket, and she missed them so fiercely right now she felt like she might cry.

"Here, I'll help you get down." Riley put his hands on Baby's waist and Baby felt a shiver of anticipation as he gently lowered her to the ground.

"So, you want to swim?" Not waiting for an answer, Riley ran into the water, goofily diving under the waves. "Come on in!" he called, in between dives.

"Wait for me! I need to get you back for the splash-fest!" Baby yelled, yanking off her T-shirt and jeans and sprinting into the ocean. She was thankful she had on her bikini. She ran in up to her chest, then splashed him hard on his back.

"Unfair. You don't hit your enemy from behind!" Riley protested, splashing her right back.

"Who says you're the enemy?" Baby teased. She felt like her lungs would explode from laughing so hard.

"Okay. So we're friends! Truce?" Riley called, holding up his hands. "To prove there's no hard feelings . . ." He gently pulled Baby into him and softly pressed his lips against hers. His mouth was cold and tasted like spearmint toothpaste.

"No hard feelings," Baby murmured, kissing him back. Her heart thudded crazily against her chest. She was hooking up with her future *sister's* boyfriend. This was wrong. This was cheating. This felt so *good*.

Forbidden love *is* the hottest. . . .

"Wait." Baby pulled away urgently. She knew that she should have done it much sooner. "What about Layla?"

Riley took a step back and stared down at the turquoise water. "We've been together since high school, and ever since we got to college, we've had this sort of understood 'don't ask, don't tell' rule. We're great friends. But things between us . . . aren't right," he began, dragging a hand over the water's smooth surface. "Things a vacation can't fix. I think we're both ready to move on, but we don't know quite how to say goodbye. Our days are numbered," he finished, his words like a sigh. There was a sadness in his eyes, but as he raised them toward Baby, also a hint of hope.

Baby considered this. Over the last few days, all she'd seen Riley and Layla do was bicker or ignore each other. Layla had told her that they met in high school, at boarding school in New Hampshire, and had stayed together for the last two years while Layla went to Oberlin and Riley went to Ithaca. She knew that distance often took its toll, and that sometimes people did stay together for the wrong reasons, even when things weren't right. But while she wanted to believe him, something was still nagging at her.

He stepped closer to Baby, his strong hands encircling her tiny waist. Baby could smell his wonderful mixture of sunblock, sweat, and horses. "It's not right with her, the way I feel it is with you," he whispered, his breath tickling her ear. He tilted his head to the side, and Baby instinctively knew what was coming next.

If she'd been thinking properly, she'd have told him that if he and Layla were about to break up, then they should wait. If she'd been thinking properly, she'd have ridden off into the sunset with Boots, knowing that her and Riley's time would come—when it was right.

But instead, she nodded slowly. Because she also knew she wanted Riley. And his lips.

She eagerly kissed him back.

Here comes trouble. . . .

the one time you want to get busy on vacation

Avery woke up facedown on the cool, crisp sheets of her bed at the villa. After seeing Rhys frolicking with the string bikini floozy in the pool, she'd lain in bed, sulking while listening to the lazy whir of the bamboo fan above her. She knew she was being immature and melodramatic, but she was just *so* tired of not having a boyfriend, of always being the girl people came to with their romantic problems. So excuse her for just being a teeny upset when, after honestly thinking she and Rhys had a connection, she saw him being such a *player*.

She turned on the TV, which was tuned to the hotel's program about all the cool things to do at the resort. Everything was about the romance of the island, and that was the last thing she wanted to see. Wasn't there some special package if you were single and disillusioned featuring a private cabana with a lot of chocolate, rum, and tissues?

She turned off the TV and wandered onto the wraparound deck, wishing there could be a rainstorm or a tornado or a monsoon—anything to match her foul mood. Instead, it was warm and sunny, and off in the distance, she could see dolphins diving into the water. She sighed and made her way back inside. Maybe she should just spend the weekend reading *Jane Eyre*, which she'd been assigned for AP English. Reading about someone whose life sucked even worse than hers did might be good for her.

Avery flung open the top of her suitcase. The book was one of the few things she hadn't bothered to unpack. She figured she'd read it on the plane ride home, after her fabulous weekend of fun and sun.

She picked up the book and flopped down on the bed. Suddenly, she heard a knock. Great. It was probably the maid service, and even the *maid* would think Avery was a loser for hanging out by herself.

"One second!" she called, adjusting the strap of her dress as she slid open the door.

There, standing sunburned and sweaty in a pair of light green board shorts and a gray T-shirt, was Rhys. What the hell?

"Hi," Avery said shortly, resisting every urge to close the door right back in his face. She couldn't *believe* she'd ever liked him.

"Hey," Rhys said warmly, totally oblivious to Avery's foul mood. "I was hoping you'd be here. What are you up to?"

"I'm busy," Avery said tightly, still holding on to the handle of the sliding door. "I'm *reading*," she added, unnecessarily holding up her book.

"Oh." Rhys's face fell. Why was he acting so oblivious? Didn't he have skanks to kiss?

"You seemed pretty busy, too, this morning," Avery spat. "I mean, have fun with your *friends*, Rhys," she amended. There. That was better. She tried to slide the door closed, but Rhys's leather Reef sandal held it open.

"Avery, are you okay? Is this about the engagement thing?" His voice was warm and concerned, and his hand fluttered upward, as if he were going to push Avery's hair back from her face. Then, abruptly, his hand fell so that it was dangling awkwardly by his belt loops.

"I don't want to talk about my family with you," Avery said. "Seriously, go back to your *friends*," she repeated. She was trying to stay angry, but the faint scent of his Clarins SPF for Men lotion and the way his eyebrows were still knit in consternation below his prominent brow was melting her resolve.

"What friends?" Rhys asked in confusion. "Are you talking about Owen?"

"No, I'm not talking about Owen," Avery blurted in frustration. "Look, it's your vacation, hook up, have fun. I mean, it's not like we did anything. I just thought you'd be classier than that." Avery cringed as soon as the words left her mouth. She sounded like a jilted Greenwich housewife, yelling at her husband after hearing a lame excuse about why he missed the train to Connecticut.

"Oh my God, those British girls? That's Owen's thing. He thought we should meet girls to sort of start fresh after Kelsey. I know it's dumb." Rhys opened his hands wide, as if to prove to her he wasn't hiding anything. "I don't know, it was a lame guy bonding idea. But I didn't like them."

Avery searched Rhys's face. It was turning bright red, and something about his wide-eyed, deer-in-headlights look made her pretty certain he wasn't lying. And he sort of looked cute when he was flustered. Still, she waited for him to finish his excuse. "Owen's crazy protective, so I couldn't tell him what's really going on. . . . What I mean is . . . I can't tell him that

I don't want those girls, because I only want *you*," Rhys finished.

"Why should I believe you?" Avery kept her hand firmly on the sliding door, as if she might suddenly slam it against Rhys's foot.

"Because I had a dream about you," Rhys said randomly, wondering why he'd chosen that of all reasons to prove his innocence. Still, it was the truth. He looked over at a terra-cotta planter in the shape of a whale that was on the patio, afraid to meet Avery's gaze.

"Okay," Avery said in what she hoped was an appropriately ice-queen voice. She turned and walked toward the kitchen. "Come in if you want."

"Thanks." Avery heard the squeaking sound of the door being pulled shut. Even though her back was toward Rhys, the room suddenly felt that much smaller.

"What was your dream about?" Avery asked, her back still toward him. She suddenly felt shy. She'd had crushes on boys before, but nothing like this. And no guy had *ever* told her he'd had a dream about her, except Dewey Williams, a kid in kindergarten who wet his pants and also had six imaginary friends. That didn't count.

But *this* did.

"It was about you," Rhys said, coming up in front of her. "You and me doing this." He cupped Avery's chin and pulled her forward. He leaned in and kissed her gently on the mouth. Avery kissed back, slowly at first, then faster. He was a few inches taller than her, and she could feel his muscled arms.

"This is better than my dream," Rhys whispered into Avery's hair. Avery nodded eagerly. She'd never made out in a hotel room, but suddenly it felt like the most natural thing in the world. Maybe Baby, Layla, and Jack could find somewhere else to sleep tonight so that she and Rhys could do this for the rest of the trip.

They'll love that plan.

Their kissing became more forceful and Avery pulled Rhys over to the couch. She sank down onto it, inviting him to sit next to her, when there was a knock on the door. Ugh. *Now* the maid decided to show up? Avery wished she'd put the DO NOT DISTURB sign on the door handle.

"Not a good time!" Avery called in between kisses. The knocks got louder. "Um, privacy? Come back later!" Avery yelled again.

"Ave, I just need to pee!" Owen yelled. "I can't make it to my room!"

"Go in the ocean!" Avery yelled. It was what Owen always used to do. Rhys clapped his hand over his mouth to suppress a laugh.

"Ave?" Owen pleaded outside. Rhys shrugged, as if to say, *What can you do?*

"*Hide!*" Avery hissed, pushing him into the bedroom and shoving the door closed. Once Rhys was out of sight, she pulled open the door to the villa.

"Hi!" Owen yelled, running into the bathroom.

A minute later, he came out, wiping his hands on the legs of his board shorts. "Hey sis," Owen said as he sauntered over to the black-and-white-striped daybed in the corner and sat down, as if settling in for an all-day chat.

"What are you up to?" Avery asked, smoothing her orange-and-green Lilly Pulitzer halter dress. She hoped she didn't look like she'd been making out.

"You know, the usual. Scoping out the scenery, meeting new

people . . ." Owen sighed and crossed his arms over his chest. "What about you? Haven't seen you around."

"Oh, well, Jack's here. So I was on the beach with her for a while. . . ."

"Really?" Owen scanned the room. "Jack's here?"

Avery instantly wished she hadn't told Owen that Jack had arrived. Of course he'd figure it out eventually, but now he was going to have a million questions. Back when the two of them had been pretending to date, she'd sensed that there was something between them, and she wasn't sure how she felt about that—especially since Jack had a boyfriend now. Besides, this was *not* the time for a sibling heart-to-heart.

"No," Avery said shortly. "She's still at the beach." She noticed Rhys's flip-flops and quickly kicked them under the couch. Owen regarded her curiously. "I think those are Layla's or Riley's. Anyway, I should take a shower, so you should probably go."

"You seem weird. Are you okay?" Owen asked, making no motion to stand up. "No!" Avery screeched. "I mean, I'm fine. I was just napping so I'm a little out of it. It's this thing where you're supposed to nap for ten minutes in the afternoon so you can stay up later. I figured vacation was the best time to try it out!" Avery said. Even as she said it, she knew it sounded absurd.

"That sounds lame." Owen wrinkled his nose and wandered into the kitchen. He rifled through the minibar and pulled out a Nature Valley granola bar. He pulled the wrapper open and took a large bite. "You haven't seen Rhys, have you?" Small flecks of crumbs sprayed onto the marble floor. Gross. Avery was very glad Rhys didn't seem to have the same terrible eating habits as her brother.

"Rhys?" she repeated dumbly.

"Yeah," Owen said ultra-slowly, as if Avery were a very slow four-year-old. He loudly crunched the rest of his granola bar. "He's been acting sort of weird. I think it's just that it's romantic here, and he's reminded of Kelsey. Does that make sense?" He frowned.

"Can we talk about this later?" Avery pleaded, practically driving Owen toward the door.

"He's just a good guy. I want him to find a good girl, you know?" Owen mused as he stood in the doorframe.

"Maybe he's looking for you. Both of the golf carts are gone," Avery said desperately. She started to literally push him out the door.

"I guess so. Okay, thanks, Ave!" Owen walked out onto the patio.

Avery breathed a sigh of relief once the door had closed behind him.

"Apparently, I need to find a good girl?" Rhys asked, pushing open the door to the bedroom. There was a teasing smirk on his face. "For a second, I was worried I'd have to hide under the bed. I actually practiced hiding there, just to make sure I'd fit," he said with a grin, his dark curls sexily tousled. Avery burst out laughing, imagining Rhys trying to wedge under the king-size bed amidst all the girls' luggage.

"When I was little I used to be scared that monsters were hiding under the bed," Avery admitted shyly. She sat on the couch and pulled her legs under her.

"Me too," Rhys confided, sliding onto the couch next to her. She looked so sweet and innocent, and it was so cute to listen to her trying to hide him from Owen. He leaned in to kiss her.

Just then, Rhys's cell beeped.

Happy T-giving, fucker. Seal the deal! Next to it was a picture of two turkeys in a lewd position. Hugh. Rhys quickly pressed delete and slid the phone back into his pocket before Avery could see it.

"Who was that?" Avery asked curiously. "One of your secret girlfriends?" she teased.

"Nothing. Just a guy from the swim team," Rhys said hoarsely. He quickly stood up, went to the door, and clicked the brass lock. *Now* they wouldn't be bothered.

"No more interruptions," Avery murmured. She tossed her long hair over her shoulder.

"Nope," Rhys whispered, hoping Avery didn't notice his phone continuing to vibrate from his pocket.

What she doesn't know can't hurt her . . . yet.

sisterly bonding

Baby dashed toward the villa on Friday evening. She and Riley had bumped into Rhys and Owen on their way back from the stables. Apparently, Owen was hell-bent on having a guys' night out at the resort's bar, and Riley had opted to join them. It was just as well: All Baby wanted was a nice hot shower.

To wash away the guilt?

She and Riley had spent all afternoon on the other side of the island, riding the horses from one cove to the next, playing in the water, and kissing. It had been so fun and magical, but part of Baby felt guilty. Riley's explanation of his and Layla's relationship made sense—she'd heard of lots of couples who did that in college—but there was a difference between making out with a random girl Layla would never meet and making out with Layla's almost stepsister.

"Hello?" Baby called as she slid open the glass door.

"Hey!" Layla emerged from the bedroom, wearing an oversize white American Apparel T-shirt belted as a dress. "How was riding?"

Baby blushed. "It was good. Um. We missed you," Baby lied.

Layla nodded. "I'm glad you and Riley had fun," she said

slowly. Baby blinked. Did Layla sound suspicious? She couldn't tell from her tone. "Your sister and her friend are getting ready for dinner. They're going to that fancy restaurant in the hotel and pretending they're ninety." Layla cracked a grin.

"I heard that!" Avery yelled from the other side of the closed bedroom door.

Baby grinned at Layla.

"Anyway, I was thinking maybe we could grab some beers and hit the beach?" Layla asked hopefully. "I feel like we haven't spent that much time together."

"That sounds great," Baby said, a lump in her throat. She was surprised to find she *did* want to spend time with Layla. She was funny and easygoing. She even got along with Avery. But the guilt over Riley felt like it was seeping out of Baby's pores.

"Great, let's go. Bye, ladies!" Layla called as she scooped up a woven hemp bag filled with cans of Kalik beers she'd obviously stolen from the guys' villa. She grabbed Baby with her other arm, and the two of them walked companionably down the limestone steps toward the beach.

"I'm really glad we're almost sisters," Baby said shyly as they settled on a piece of driftwood and gazed toward the horizon. It was true. No matter what, this afternoon had to be a one-time thing. No matter what their relationship agreement was, it definitely didn't apply to *sisters*.

But what about stepsisters?

"Me too. I've always wanted a little sister." Layla grinned and cracked open two beers.

"I never thought about that." Baby glanced at Layla's profile. She was so pretty, with her curly hair piled high on the top of her head. She was obviously the type of girl who only did what made her happy and only spent time with people she liked. What would happen when she found out her little sister had made out with her boyfriend? Baby shivered at the thought.

"Cold?" Layla asked. She rooted through her hemp bag, pulled out an oversize purple hoodie, and offered it to Baby.

"I'm good. So, Layla? Is that from the Eric Clapton song?" Baby asked shyly.

"How'd you guess?" Layla rolled her eyes, as if that was what everyone asked her about her name. Baby winced in sympathy. She could understand. Everyone who met her assumed her name was from *Dirty Dancing*. Layla shrugged and took a sip of her beer.

Layla cleared her throat. "It's funny. My dad's always been so into music and art, but growing up, all he cared about was work. It's only been in the past couple years that he's seemed to really like his life. I always want to like my life, you know?"

"Me too," Baby admitted. She pushed her small feet farther into the cool sand.

"That's my first piece of big-sister advice." Layla grinned, but her tone was serious. "In high school, I thought I knew who I was. And then in college, you learn so much about yourself. I mean, yeah, that sounds totally lame, but you sort of find out who you really are, away from your family and friends. Of course, I always had Riley. . . ." Layla trailed off.

"Did that make going to college easier?" Baby asked finally, unsure of what to say that wouldn't sound like it was prying.

How considerate.

"Yes and no. It's hard because I sometimes wonder what it would have been like if I came to college totally single. I sometimes think I'm ready to take the plunge and dive out of the nest or whatever that saying is," Layla confessed, looking into the horizon. The sun was slowly setting. Waves gently lapped at the shore.

Baby's heartbeat quickened. Did that mean that *Layla* thought she and Riley were over? "When I moved to the city from Nantucket, I stayed with my boyfriend for a little," Baby offered.

"What happened?"

"He cheated on me and we broke up," Baby admitted, a shiver running up her spine. Thinking about it, wasn't that *exactly* the same thing going on between Layla and Riley? Baby shivered, not liking where this conversation was going. After all, it was a totally different situation. Tom had been a pot-smoking high school boy. Riley was a sensitive artist. It was totally different.

Totally.

"What's Oberlin like?" Baby asked, desperately trying to change the subject.

"It's fine." Layla sighed. "No, it's great. I love my classes and my friends and my music, and it's almost like everything I ever wanted. It's just sometimes hard to grow up and do what you have to do," she added cryptically.

Baby gazed out on the ocean. The sun was reflecting on the water, making it look like the water was on fire. Layla was sweet and sincere, and a large part of Baby wanted to tell her about what had happened on the beach with Riley this afternoon. But then she remembered Riley's lopsided smile and the way he kissed her and his adorable Texas accent . . .

And the fact he calls himself a Player?

"Dude, I'm freaking starving!" Layla said, the mood broken. "I think the bar by the pool has some fried conch. Wanna share?" She smiled warmly at Baby.

Sharing *is* caring.

announcement

Saturday afternoon, Avery ran into Le Sel de Mer, the lavish dining room in the main hotel. She weaved past bored-looking couples picking at their plates of tuna tartare and gossiping about the Gstaad ski vacations they were planning for Christmas. She scanned the room but couldn't see her mother's elephant-batiked sarong or Birkenstocks amid the women dressed in silk pastel dresses.

"Hey!" Baby called from a center table, waving Avery over. Her hair was pulled in two messy braids on either side of her head and she was wearing an oversize white linen shirt belted as a dress. She looked ridiculously cool, even while she was shredding her iced-tea straw wrapper into smaller and smaller pieces.

"Hi," Avery said cautiously as she sat down in one of the wicker chairs opposite Baby. Something seemed off about her ever since last night. She hoped she wasn't still mad about Jack being here.

"Hi." Baby didn't look up from her iced tea. "What have you been up to this morning?" she asked quickly, as if sensing that Avery was about to launch an open investigation into her emotions. After she and Layla had their heart-to-heart last night, Baby had faked sick from the fried conch and had gone to bed early. She had a lot to think about. What she and Riley had done during the afternoon had seemed so right, and had even made sense, especially when Riley explained his and Layla's "don't ask, don't tell" policy. But it got complicated when she factored in how much she *liked* Layla.

"Nothing much." Now it was Avery's turn to block any future questions. She loved keeping her and Rhys's relationship a secret. It was romantic, sort of like in *Titanic*, which Avery would never admit she actually loved. Except it was *better*, since she and Rhys didn't have any of those pesky class differences to navigate.

Avery spread her daffodil yellow napkin over her lap. "Where's Layla?"

"I'm here." Layla glided over to the table, her Coach sunglasses perched atop her curls. "You okay?" she asked Baby, ruffling her tousled brown hair. "Riley asked about you this morning. I had to indulge him by going on another pony ride." Layla rolled her large green eyes.

"Yeah." Baby stammered. "I mean, it was just the food. I got sick because of the food." Baby was speaking way too quickly, using the same voice she'd used when she was trying to tell Avery she hadn't stolen her favorite Citizen skinny jeans. Avery narrowed her eyes. *What* was going on?

"I thought it was fine," Layla said easily. "Probably because I'm used to dining hall food. Seriously, college gives you a stomach of steel," she said knowingly.

"Oh look!" Edie's unmistakable voice pierced the air. Avery looked up and saw her mom wearing a sand-colored maxidress that looked like it was made out of a discarded ship sail, dragging

Remington behind her. Remington was wearing the same white linen pants and white linen shirt he'd worn yesterday. "They're all together!" Edie stood for a moment and stared at them, obviously taking in the scene for future artistic reference.

Avery smiled. Despite their weird hippie-holiday attire, her mom and Remington looked good together. More than that, she'd never seen her mom so happy. It was obvious she was in love.

It runs in the family!

"My brood!" Edie swooped down and kissed the top of Avery, Baby, and Layla's heads. "You're bonding!" she cooed fondly, completely oblivious to the fact the whole restaurant was regarding her curiously. "Don't they look great?" she asked the gray-haired restaurant host, who was patiently clutching a collection of woven straw menus in his hands.

"Lovely," the host murmured politely. He pulled one of the chairs out for Edie.

"Thank you," Edie said as she sat down with a noisy clatter.

"So, what's happening with you all?" she asked as if she were an ultra-caffeinated morning talk show host.

"Not too much," Avery said after a moment of silence. "Jack and I are having fun. She's hanging on the beach."

"I'm so glad she decided to come stay with us," Edie said absently as she threaded her fingers into Remington's.

"That's great." Remington nodded. "You know, for so many years, I forgot how great it is to just gather people around. Have a party!" He nodded happily.

A white apron–clad man wearing a light blue freshly pressed Mao-collared jacket strode over to the table. "You, sir, are in trouble," he said, shaking his head at Remington. "I'm Jean Luc, the chef here," the man explained to the girls. "I've been here for years, and this gentleman used to be one of our best customers. Here all the time, life of the party! But then he has a midlife crisis, goes to find himself—I don't know where better to find yourself than in paradise, but who am I to say?" the chef asked, of no one in particular. "But I have to say, I'm just glad you found your way back and with such beautiful guests. I'm sending over the tasting menu and some dark and stormies to your party. Even though now you're Mister Light and Sunny!" Jean Luc smiled as Remington laughed and jumped up to give his old friend a hearty handshake.

"Oh, Remy, you were never dark and stormy. Except for those business school years when I'd run into you." Edie shook her head, enjoying her private recollection. Avery shifted in her seat. Yes, she was happy for them, but couldn't they stop talking and eat lunch?

"Let's keep the dark and stormy side out of it," Remington laughed, then leaned in and kissed the tip of Edie's ski-jump nose, giving it a playful bite.

"Daddy, you're embarrassing!" Layla squealed, but it didn't sound like she really minded.

"I'm embarrassing?" Remington roared playfully. "I have to watch you and Riley cozying up to each other all the time." He clapped Layla on the back. "Just a little payback to my dear daughter."

"Can I be excused for a second?" Baby asked, pushing her chair back.

"Of course, sweet!" Edie said. "I hope you're not still sick," she fretted.

"I'll make sure she's all right." Avery scraped her chair back.

Why was Baby acting so weird? Avery had never seen her so nervous, not even on the many occasions she was called to the headmistress's office at Constance. She hoped that she didn't have a problem with Remington, the way Owen seemed to.

Avery pushed open the white wooden door to the women's bathroom and saw Baby sitting on a pearly pink ottoman and gazing miserably into the seashell-framed mirror opposite her.

"What's going on?" Avery put her hands on her hips and glared down at her tiny sister.

"Nothing. I think I need to lie down, though. I'm definitely still not over my bug." Baby nodded, as if trying to convince herself. "Can you tell them that I'm so happy they're happy, and that I'll talk to them later? I'll even do whatever tropical fun activity Mom wants," Baby said breathlessly. She smiled, but Avery could tell something was off about Baby. And it probably wasn't food poisoning. Baby *never* got sick, even when she ate hot dogs from street cart vendors.

The bathroom door burst open. An elderly lady carrying two small King Charles spaniels under each arm glared at them in disapproval.

"Are you done gossiping in here?" she asked. "Because they need some privacy," she said, glancing down at the dogs.

Avery smiled, knowing that was totally the type of random thing Baby would love. But Baby didn't catch her eye.

"Sorry, ma'am!" Baby said, and quickly ran out of the bathroom.

Avery sighed and washed her hands under the cool water of the sink. If a vacation was supposed to be relaxing, why was everyone acting so uptight?

Back in the dining room, the table was covered with cerulean blue platters piled high with different types of fish. Remington was already digging into his meal, lustily sucking out a lobster claw and wearing a blue bib around his neck.

"You're back!" he called, cheerily waving the lobster claw in greeting.

"Where's Baby?" Edie asked, a hint of worry entering her usually breathy tone.

"Still not feeling well." Avery shrugged. "She went to take a nap."

Layla pushed her salad around her plate. "I think it was the combo of fried food and beers last night." Layla wrinkled her nose.

"Stop that talk!" Edie said, waving her hand as if to dismiss the notion entirely. "It's not your fault at all. I know she thinks the world of you." Edie grinned at Layla fondly.

"She's a good kid, that one. And so are you, Avery," Remington said magnanimously as he took a bite of his lobster. "You know, I know I've only known you and Baby for a bit, but I like to think of you girls as my daughters," he said. "And I know it's a process, and I'm certainly not going to come in and uproot your lives. I like all of you just the way you are."

Thank you, Mr. Rogers.

"You know what?" Edie interrupted, setting her knife and fork down with a loud clatter. "I don't want to spend the next few months talking about the *process* of becoming a family. Remington, let's just get married now. Here, at the resort. *Carpe diem!*" She was practically shouting. The hum of the room quieted, so all that could be heard was Edie and the whir of the fans above them. Even the bartenders had stopped making drinks and were standing, shakers in midair.

Avery dropped her fork and Remington turned to her with a bemused smile on his face. One of the tuxedoed servers picked it up off the floor and discreetly tucked it away.

Avery caught Layla's eye. She had the same *what the fuck?* expression Avery was sure was on her own face. Married? *Now?* How? There was no dress, no flowers, no time!

"Spontaneity. This is why I love this woman! Edie, you are absolutely right, this is the perfect place and time to get married. Let's do it, babe." Remington leaned across the table and kissed Edie. The entire restaurant, not knowing what else to do, broke into spontaneous applause. A parade of waiters came out with two bottles of champagne and proceeded to pour glasses for everyone at the table. Even Remington's chef friend had a tear in his eye.

Only because they upstaged his Michelin-starred cuisine.

"You can't get married!" Avery began. Layla shot her a sympathetic glance. "No, I mean, I want you guys to get married if you want to, but you need time! You can't just do these things," Avery said bossily. A wedding should be at St. Patrick's Cathedral with a reception at the Plaza or the Waldorf or at least a classy sit-down dinner at the Four Seasons.

"Nonsense." Edie shook her head, clearly amused by her daughter. "I'm not some twenty-six-year-old. I don't want a lot of guests—I just want my family. Oooh, maybe we could get those steel-drum players. Do you think they do Peter, Paul, and Mary?"

Avery couldn't believe what she was hearing. Had her mother lost her mind? A steel-drum *Peter, Paul, and Mary* cover band? If her mom was so hell-bent on doing this, she needed *serious* help.

Remington chuckled. "This is the reason I love your mother," he said confidentially to Avery. "I agree with her. Besides, I've never liked weddings in New York. *Remington Wallis, whose previous marriage ended in divorce . . .*" he began, imitating the way the *New York Times* wrote its wedding coverage. "Nope. We can fly in some of the art folk, but that's about it," Remington said, warming up to the idea.

"I have a white sarong and Baby could take photos, and of course, Riley and Layla could sing," Edie mused. "Like what was the one we listened to at the Grateful Dead concert? The one where you wouldn't smoke pot, but you bought ice cream for everyone afterward? I think that was when we were sophomores. It was when we drove up to Vermont in that old Cougar?" Edie's eyes misted over at the memory.

"Mom," Avery said firmly. Edie looked up expectantly from her bite of snapper, as if surprised Avery was still stuck on the topic. "Please let me help you? You need a dress. And flowers. And I'll plan the meal, and I'll make it nice. Not over-the-top," she added.

"But this is our vacation, darling. I don't want any fuss." Edie knit her brows together in consternation.

"It's no trouble. It'll be fun."

"You know, if she wants to, let her do it. She's got a great eye." Remington winked at her. "And while she does that, don't you think I should go talk to Owen?" Remington asked, his voice laced with concern.

"Of course." Edie grinned. "I think it'd be great if you two got to know each other a bit more."

Avery smiled shyly at her new family. Okay, so it was weird and random, but, honestly, her *mom* was weird and random. And, no matter what, she was going to make this work.

In between make-out sessions with Rhys, of course.

fancy meeting you here

Saturday afternoon, Jack relaxed on her chaise longue on the stretch of beach behind the villas. Avery was having lunch at the resort's restaurant with her mom and sister, and Jack had politely declined, not wanting to intrude on the family affair.

Avery had disappeared all afternoon yesterday, taking a ridiculously long nap, but last night she and Jack had had fun, going out to dinner at the hotel and then getting drinks at the hotel bar while silver-haired businessmen attempted to talk them up. Jack had spent the whole evening hoping Owen might show up, but he must have been off on his bachelor evening with Rhys and Riley . . . or he was holed up in his skank girlfriend's room.

Jack flipped over onto her back. She definitely hadn't planned on spending this vacation alone, but at the same time, the quiet was sort of nice. The sun was high above the ocean, casting a goldfish-colored haze on the water.

Back in New York, she and J.P. used to watch the sun rise a lot. Whenever she'd crashed at his apartment after a party, when she didn't feel like dealing with her annoying mom, he'd poke her awake at 5 a.m. and drag her up to his private terrace. She wasn't much of a morning person, so he'd always have a latte with extra sugar—her favorite. He'd been the type of guy who could still be friendly and happy after only four hours of sleep. In a lot of ways, he was perfect.

Jack sighed, imagining what things would be like when she got back to the city in a few days. J.P. had been disappointed when she'd let him know about her plans to go to the Bahamas, but of course he understood. He always did. That was the problem: Everything between them was so *predictable*. It was as if she could already see the path her life would take. She'd become a professional dancer while juggling classes at Columbia, while J.P. would go to Yale and come visit her on the weekends. Then they'd get married at St. Patrick's Cathedral, have a lavish reception at the Waldorf, then settle into the Cashman Complexes in Tribeca. Once her dance career was over, they'd move to one of the more family-friendly Cashman properties on the Upper East Side. J.P. would work for his dad, she'd chair benefits for the New York City Ballet and monitor the activities of their three kids, who would be spaced apart by two and a half years. And so on.

Before, this vision of her life had cheered her. But now it just felt boring, staid, predictable. Suffocating, even.

Jack didn't want to think about it anymore. She leaned back on the chair, closed her eyes, and yanked her Gucci aviators down. The sound of the ocean and the warm sun caused her to fall asleep almost instantly.

"Hey!"

Jack blinked open her eyes and found Owen staring down at her. Immediately she sat up, hoping she hadn't done anything embarrassing like drool all over herself. Owen was shirtless, and sweat glistened on his bronzed chest. But instead of grossing her out, it was kind of sexy, like he'd stepped out of a *GQ* spread.

Or out of her dreams.

"Hey," Owen said gently. "You shouldn't just fall asleep on the beach. It's not safe." He gingerly perched on the edge of the deck chair. He knew Jack had gotten here yesterday, but this was the first time he'd actually laid eyes on her. She looked sleepy and wasn't wearing any makeup, but her bikini top was ever so slightly askew, exposing a half-inch more chest than was strictly decent. All in all, Jack looked totally bed-head hot. Owen couldn't help but wonder what it would be like to wake up next to her.

"I know. I just closed my eyes and I must have fallen asleep." Jack hiked up her green Eres bikini to make sure she wasn't flashing him. She glanced again at his sweaty chest. "You're really into working out, huh?" she asked. J.P. played squash and golf, and rowed crew, but he always seemed to do it with a sense of obligation. Owen just seemed to be a more physical person.

"Not always." Owen shrugged. "I like running when I need to think, though."

"Is everything okay?" Jack asked, looking concerned. Owen gazed at her flawless face. Her green eyes almost matched her green bikini and sarong. It tied at the hip, and Owen struggled to push aside dirty thoughts about undoing the knot.

"No, I mean, I just have a lot on my mind," Owen explained. Ever since he'd realized yesterday that he'd never had real feelings for Kelsey, his head had been spinning. *Was* he a player? Did he really just see girls as sex? And was he ever going to be in a real relationship? His mom announcing her engagement to Remington had been messing with his head. After all, Edie had always been single—how did she just *know* Remington was the one? And how much did she really know about him? Owen was used to being overprotective of his sisters, but he was also protective of his mom. He didn't want her to get hurt. "I feel like back home there's so much going on. It's hard to think in New York, you know. How do you do it?" Owen finished lamely, settling down into the chaise next to Jack. He probably sounded like a complete lunatic.

But she didn't seem to think that was a crazy question at all. "Think in the city? You get used to it. I don't know. I guess you just have to find people you can talk things out to and go from there." She shrugged and gazed out at the water.

"I'm trying to make sure my buddy Rhys is having a good time," Owen finally said. That wasn't really the whole truth, but it was a good start.

"You shouldn't be so concerned about other people. It only fucks you up. Starting with this trip, I've decided I'm *only* going to do what makes me happy for the rest of the year," Jack said definitively. "What makes *you* happy?

Owen considered. Swimming made him happy. So did kissing, Pop-Tarts, a bacon, egg, and cheese sandwich from the deli down the street, and summer thunderstorms. But all of that sounded sort of dumb.

"I guess life makes me happy," he said finally.

Deep.

Jack cracked a smile. "Life?" she asked skeptically.

"What about you?" Owen asked. He really did want to know. He knew she was a dancer and her mom was French, but other than that, he really didn't know much about Jack.

"Oh, I don't know." She sighed, sounding so world-weary that Owen was taken aback. "Ballet for sure. Summer, parks, traveling, Paris . . . It's like I don't know when I'm happy until I look back on it afterward."

Owen nodded. He knew what she meant. Back in Nantucket, he'd breezed through life, winning swim meets, getting all the girls, and not really thinking about any of it. It was only after he got to New York, and saw how complicated life could be, that he realized how good he'd had it. Not that he wanted to go back to the way things had been before. Nantucket had been great, sure, and he definitely missed his island home from time to time. But to return there would somehow feel like backtracking. He'd been through a lot of friend and romantic drama since they'd moved, but he was none the worse for wear. And things were certainly looking pretty good right now.

"What was the best day of your life?" Owen asked randomly. He leaned down and drew a smiley face in the sand with his finger, then brushed it away. It was kind of nice to just talk to a girl. That was the thing. Whenever he'd begin to get close to a girl, he'd become frustrated when he tried to talk about *real* things besides clothes and parties with her. Like Kelsey. She'd been super-artistic, and Owen had wanted to hear what inspired her. Instead, she'd always giggle and initiate a make-out session, as if the only thing that mattered between them was sex. But Jack seemed . . . different.

"I don't know." A smile played on Jack's lips. "Maybe it'll be today."

"Yeah?" Owen arched a blond eyebrow.

"Maybe." Jack shrugged. Looking into Owen's bright blue eyes, a lot of things suddenly seemed possible. He wasn't so set in his ways, like so many guys back in New York. She tried imagining a future with Owen. Maybe they wouldn't go to college. Maybe they'd backpack through India, or maybe they'd sail around the world. The possibilities seemed as endless as the ocean stretching before them.

"You want to go swimming?" Jack asked, untying the sea green pareo at her hip. She bit her coral-colored lip, as if waiting for an answer.

Owen found himself distracted by the curve of Jack's lips. *Calm the fuck down, Carlyle.* Owen reminded himself that Jack had a boyfriend. And while he couldn't deny that it had been exciting to hook up with Kelsey while she was in a relationship—the thrill of secrecy, and all that—look at where it had gotten him. He'd already been down that road before. He needed something simple and no-drama. Like Elsie, maybe. She'd been calling him all day. Maybe he should call her back.

"You coming?" Jack asked, already skipping into the water, playing in the waves. She looked graceful, with her dancer's legs.

Yeah, Owen decided, getting up and following her. He'd call Elsie back.

Later.

a plans it out

Avery marched authoritatively through the lobby of the hotel that afternoon, not even noticing the parrot that practically flew into her dress. She couldn't believe her mother was getting married *tomorrow*. There was so much work to be done! She had to find appropriate clothing for her and the girls, make sure the guys had suits, had to find music that wasn't too hippietastic, find a party planner . . . and then there was the food, the champagne, the officiant . . . Avery felt dizzy just thinking about it as she marched toward the front desk.

"I'm planning a wedding and I need to speak to a wedding planner immediately," Avery announced to the pretty woman behind the reception desk.

"Congratulations!" The receptionist's expression changed from pleasant to surprised as she gave Avery a once-over. "You're going to need to speak to Yvette. She does all our bookings. Now, she has some availability tomorrow . . ."

"The *wedding's* tomorrow!" Avery screeched. "I mean, is there any way to speak to her today? It's a small wedding," she pleaded.

The woman appraised Avery, seeming to sense she was the type of girl who wouldn't take no for an answer. "Well, if it's an emergency . . . I'll just be a second," she said to the man sitting at the computer next to her. "Come with me, darling. No tears, we'll make this a dream wedding." She squeezed Avery's upper arm reassuringly. Avery nodded. Why had she even gotten herself into this? She could be on the beach with Jack or Rhys, her new boyfriend. She couldn't help but smile when she thought about him.

She was escorted into a glass-enclosed office that reminded Avery of the offices at *Metropolitan*, the magazine where she'd interned. A harried-looking woman was barking into her cell phone. She had honey-colored hair, red cat's-eye glasses, and obvious Botox. Despite the heat, she was wearing a black St. John's suit.

"Well, I don't *care* if Rihanna doesn't do private parties. My clients want her to perform. It's the goddamn most important day of their lives, they don't really care about the money. Just tell her to make it work." She slammed down the phone and glanced curiously at Avery.

"She has a rush wedding," the receptionist explained, then scampered out, clearly terrified of Yvette.

"Tomorrow," Avery clarified, looking around the windowless office. A plate of multicolored macaroons sat on Yvette's desk, the only color in the sea of blacks and steel grays. It didn't look very celebratory.

"You young girls getting married." Yvette shook her head. "Well, we do charge additional for a *rush* ceremony, but stick with me, kid. I'll give you the wedding of your dreams. And you're in luck, because we just had a cancellation. Goddamn prick was cheating on her with her tennis instructor. Her *male* tennis instructor," the woman clucked. "You play tennis?"

"Um, no." Avery shuffled from one pink Miu Miu pump to the other. "I'm actually not getting married. It's my mother," she clarified.

"Oh." For a brief moment, Yvette looked disappointed. "Well, okay. So, religious?"

"No," Avery said quickly. Edie had gone through a pagan phase where she'd thrown parties and praised various earth goddesses, but thankfully, that was in the past.

"Number of guests?"

"Um, thirty?" Avery said, rounding up since she knew her mom's penchant for inviting random people to parties. "And we're staying over at the villas, so I was thinking we could do everything there. Maybe the reception by the pool? And I'd really like a lot of whites and candlelight. I want it to be low-key but romantic. I want it to be like a dream version of a desert island. But not cheesy. Orchids, not roses. And no crappy DJ. A jazz band, maybe." Avery nodded. Now that she thought about it, an island wedding *was* romantic. She imagined Rhys in an off-white suit and her wearing a mermaid-cut white dress, standing barefoot on the beach. Actually, not barefoot, she'd wear an adorable pair of Christian Louboutin slingbacks so Rhys would pick her up and carry her . . .

"Done!" Yvette was typing some things in the computer, yanking Avery back to reality—she wasn't planning *her* wedding, she was planning her mother's wedding.

"Honey, relax. I'm the professional. I'll give your mom the wedding she wants. Now, for payment . . ." Yvette trailed off. Avery fished in her voluminous straw Marc Jacobs bag and threw down her black AmEx card. Yvette grinned like a three-year-old on Christmas morning. "Terrific. So, you trust my judgment?"

Avery nodded. It wasn't like she had much of a choice. "What about dresses?"

"I'm calling Jasmin and having her close down the store for you. It's a big time in your family's life. Enjoy it," Yvette said, noting Avery's skeptical expression.

Ten minutes later, Avery was standing on a pedestal in the rear of the resort boutique. She'd ignored the store every time she'd walked past, sure it was full of resort clothes for middle-aged women. But it was actually sort of cool, and she loved having the whole place to herself. She sipped from a glass of champagne and glanced at the side table next to her that was covered with a fruit and cheese plate and a platter of crudités. It'd have been more fun if *anyone* was here to help her—she'd texted Jack, but with no response; she didn't have Layla's number; and when she'd called she'd gotten Baby's voice mail. Not that Baby had any interest in wedding planning. Still, there were worse ways to spend a few hours than being fawned over by an adoring salesperson.

She should tell that to her sister.

"You make the perfect bride," Jasmin, the pretty, tiny salesperson murmured.

Avery turned in the three-way mirror and examined her butt in the purple silk Chloé dress she was trying on. "I think I mentioned, it's my mom who's getting married?"

"Forgive me!" Jasmin's dark brown eyes widened. "It's just that you're so beautiful in that. You *would* make a perfect bride."

"Thanks," Avery said. The dress was pretty, but it was impossible to know if it was the *right* maid of honor dress to wear for her mom's wedding. She really wanted Jack's opinion, and wished her friend would pick up the phone. Of course, she could call Rhys, who would only be too happy to come. Since yesterday, they'd been texting nonstop. Last night, at the hotel bar with Jack, Avery had blushed and tried not to giggle as he sent her flirty text after flirty text. As the night wore on, their flirt-texting became a little more . . . intense. Make that sexual. Which got Avery excited, but also made her a little nervous. She'd never done *it* before, because she'd never met the right person. Rhys had had a girlfriend for years, so surely he had more experience. Avery wasn't worried, though. Rhys was a total gentleman. Sex was the last thing on his mind.

She took out her phone to invite him over here, but hesitated. She sort of wanted her dress to be a surprise. Wasn't it bad luck for the bride to see the groom before the wedding?

Ahem, bride and groom?

"I guess I'll take it. Actually, three of them. Two in this size," Avery decided, guessing that, even though her chest was slightly bigger and her waist was a little bit smaller, she and Layla were roughly the same size. "And one in a zero." Baby.

"Okay." Jasmin nodded. "And the wedding dress? We have one Ralph Lauren Collection piece that I think might be perfect." She led Avery to a gorgeous, flowing silk georgette dress. It wasn't a wedding dress; instead it was a knee-length cocktail dress one might wear to an elegant outdoor party. Avery fingered the slightly sheer, whisper-soft ivory material. It was perfect for her mom.

"That too."

"Great. I'll do the alterations tonight, once your mom can come in. Do you think she'll be able to make it here soon?"

"Yes," Avery said. They only had a matter of hours, but she'd just have to drag her mom to the boutique. Edie would have to tear herself away from island basket weaving, or whatever she was doing.

"Perfect." Jasmin smiled and clapped her hands. "You can really tell you're surrounded by love. You're even better than working with a bride."

Avery blushed. "Thanks!" She pushed the glass door of the boutique open and practically ran up the hill toward the villa complex. She needed to call Yvette to confirm all the details, plus she wanted to squeeze in a quick manicure, too.

"Hello?" Avery called as she yanked the door of the villa open a few hours later, dresses in hand. The villa was a total mess, with clothing and bikini tops scattered in a path toward the sliding patio door. After her whirlwind afternoon, during which she'd dragged her mom to the boutique for her alterations and basically gotten the *entire* wedding in place, she wanted a shower and a nap to rest up before the rehearsal dinner tonight—which, of course, she'd also organized. "Guys?" she called again.

"Outside!" Avery heard Owen's muffled voice through the paned glass. She could just make out two figures sitting in the hot tub, their heads tilted close to one another.

Avery made her way outside. Owen was lazing around in the hot tub, glasses of what looked like homemade dark and stormies scattered around its edge. And with him was . . . *Jack?* They were sitting close beside each other, looking awfully cozy.

Suddenly, Jack's words when she first arrived repeated on loop in Avery's head: *"I missed you so much! New York was so bor-*

ing without you!" Avery narrowed her eyes. So Jack got bored in the city, and decided to come to the Bahamas to flirt with *her* brother? All the while lying to Avery and playing the friendship card? So not cool.

"Where have you been?" Owen asked, cocking his glass tumbler toward her. "Come hang out!"

"Um, getting ready for our mother's *wedding*. Why didn't you guys answer your phones?" Avery asked hotly. She felt like stomping her foot and having a temper tantrum. Until she saw Owen's face, totally drained of color.

"Wedding?" he asked hoarsely.

"Yeah, *tomorrow*. They decided at lunch today. She didn't tell you guys?" Avery shook her head in disbelief. What the hell was her mother doing? Edie Carlyle had always been flighty, but failing to mention her rapidly impending wedding seemed a little extreme, even for her.

"What the fuck?" Owen stepped out of the hot tub, sloshing water all over the sandstone patio.

"Well, you should have answered your phone. Or looked at your texts," Avery retorted, briefly losing patience. She knew Owen was having some issues with Remington, but she *really* didn't want to play family therapist. There was too much *real* work to be done.

"Sorry, Avery. We were hanging out in the hot tub, so we didn't have our phones." Jack clambered out of the hot tub too, looking perfect and taut in a green Eres bikini that matched her eyes. "But that's great, right?"

"Yeah, great," Avery said, stalking back into the hotel room. Her mother was getting married in less than twenty-four hours, her brother was having some freaky Oedipal crisis, and her best friend was obviously only here to hook up with her brother. *Fan-fucking-tastic.*

Avery walked back into the villa, feeling deflated. The dresses were hanging on a clothing rack in the center of the room, making it look like a boutique outpost. She took one of the white garment bags and brought it over to the closet.

"Is that what you're going to wear? Can I see?" Jack asked as she entered the room. She was re-tying her bathing suit top around her neck, and Avery really hoped she hadn't been topless in the hot tub.

"No," Avery said shortly. Why did Jack always make everything about her? "I mean, you're all wet. I don't want the fabric to stain," she lied.

"Sorry!" Jack skulked over to the couch, leaving a trail of water in her wake. "And I'm really sorry I didn't answer your texts. Obviously, I would have if I hadn't been—"

"Flirting with my brother?" Avery asked, whirling around to face Jack. It was annoying that Jack was going after Owen. But that wasn't even the problem. It was the fact that Jack a) had a *boyfriend,* and b) had *lied* to Avery about why she came down from New York. "Tell me honestly: Is that why you came here? For him, not me?"

"I came here because . . ." Jack trailed off. Why *had* she come here? It was true that she wanted Owen; with every minute they spent together, she became more and more sure that there was really something there. But that wasn't the only reason, and it certainly wasn't one she was going to share with Avery, when her friend was clearly in a mood. "My friends were being annoying, the stepbrats were driving me up the wall, and J.P. was being totally predictable," Jack answered honestly. "I just needed a change of scene."

Avery regarded her friend. Jack sat on the couch, hugging her knees to her chest. She looked very small and vulnerable. Still, Avery knew Jack was an expert in manipulation. "Is there anything I can do to help you now?" Jack asked, sounding defensive.

"No," Avery said coldly. "I think it's better if just family is involved."

"Okay, call me if you need me." Jack walked back onto the terrace, leaving Avery alone.

She felt momentarily bad, especially since Jack had such a fucked-up family of her own. But still. It was one thing to have a crush on her brother—a lot of people did. But to lie to Avery's face about it . . . She seriously hoped Jack was telling her the truth.

And she seriously should know better.

the young man and the sea

"She fucking decides to marry him tomorrow? Who the fuck does that?" Owen paced back and forth through the villa, trying to make a trail through the T-shirts, empty beer bottles, and potato chip bags scattered on the floor. By the second morning, Rhys had given up cleaning the shared space. He was half-asleep on the couch right now, while Riley picked out a song on his guitar.

"Dude, that's more notice than I had for my mom's second marriage. She got married in Vegas to a bus driver." Riley shrugged, his guitar slung over his chest. "Besides, Remington's cool. At least he supports the arts."

"Whatever." Owen didn't want to hear it. It was one thing for his mom to be engaged. Knowing her, she'd probably never actually get around to getting married. They still hadn't even *unpacked* their NYC penthouse yet. But to get married *tomorrow*? And to have this former banker, this faux patron of the arts be, like, his *dad*?

Daddy issues rear their ugly head.

"Owen?" a male voice called from outside.

"Busy," Owen called, glaring at Riley, who was mid-step toward answering the door.

"I come with beers!" Remington yelled through the door. Great. So now he was going to be buddy-buddy with them. He might as well just move into the guys' villa and set up a beer-pong table while he was at it.

And that would be a bad thing?

"One second, sir!" Riley called, kicking some empty Kalik beer cans under the wicker coffee table. "What? We're low on booze. Especially the way you're going through it," he remarked to Owen, sliding open the door. Remington stepped over the teenage boy debris. "I see the maid's been here," he cracked lamely. Owen refused to look at him.

"So, your mom is making us official," Remington said, sitting down on the love seat and glancing around as if he expected Owen to give him a high five or something.

"It's certainly a surprise," Owen said stiffly, balling his hands into the pockets of his board shorts. He sort of felt like hitting Remington in his self-satisfied face.

"Congratulations, sir!" Rhys leapt up and stuck out his hand, and Riley quickly followed suit. *Traitors.*

"Thanks." Remington pumped Rhys's hand enthusiastically. "Riley, I'd be honored if you and my little girl would put together some music to set the mood. Also, I was going to take *Sounder* out for a spin, just for a little while before dinner tonight. I'd love it if you would join me."

Owen frowned. *Sounder?* Who was that? A bimbo ex-girlfriend?

"My yacht," Remington explained. "I keep it docked here, but I don't use it much. Since I sold the property, I just haven't felt the call of the ocean. What do you guys think?" he asked, looking around hopefully.

"Well, I should work on a set list for the wedding," Riley said.

"I've got to, um, do some stuff," Rhys stammered. Quickly, the two guys walked outside, Riley taking the six-pack Remington had brought with him. Owen smiled tightly. Great. Now it was just the two of them.

"Look, son—I mean, Owen," Remington said, hastily correcting himself. He sounded more nervous than Owen had ever heard him, even when he'd asked Edie to marry him. "I'm not your dad. I think you're a great guy. Let's just get to know each other. I do have some great Cuban cigars on board," he offered.

Owen sighed. Any excuse was useless. Remington wasn't going to leave him alone. "Okay," he heard himself saying.

"Here she is," Remington said proudly as he gestured to a thirty-foot yacht bobbing up and down on the blue sea. A driver had brought them to the other side of the island, to a small marina filled with yachts, each one larger than the last. "Named her after my first dog." Owen furrowed his brows. His first *dog*? Honestly, this guy was so weird, he could kind of see why his mom liked him.

They stepped onto the deck, where a team of three skinny crewmembers wearing blue cotton shirts with *Sounder* embroidered on the breast in gold script eagerly greeted Remington.

"Good to be back," Remington said with a twinkle in his eye as he led Owen to the cabin. There, he and another crewmember busied themselves with the navigational system. "There are some beers and snacks in the kitchen. Grab whatever you'd like."

Owen poked into the kitchen, which was stocked with oysters, Osetra caviar, rum, Oregon Coast beers, and mangos. At least Remington had good taste in snacks. Owen cracked open a beer and walked unsteadily back to the cabin. Maybe he could fake seasickness.

"I love these islands," Remington said after a moment, not seeming to care that Owen hadn't bothered to bring him a beer. He turned and led them both to the stern of the boat and pulled out a few fishing rods from under a bench. "Hemingway did too."

"That's great, sir," Owen said gruffly. He couldn't believe he'd left the hot tub with a bikini-clad Jack to talk about Hemingway.

"Here you go." Remington passed him a pre-baited rod and reel and settled back on the cushioned bench. "I used to always want to be a writer. Or an artist. That's what I really love about your mom. She just goes after what she wants."

"Um," Owen grunted. The line on his fishing rod tightened. Maybe he'd catch a shark and it would eat Remington. His family had been *fine* on its own for sixteen years. He'd been fine—more than fine—with just his mom and his sisters. And now this guy was going to come in and give him some life lecture?

"You know, I thought I'd missed my chance at happiness. I met your mom when we were so young, and she was so vibrant, so alive. I was terrified of her, mainly because I knew she wouldn't put up with the money-is-power bullshit I was feeding myself. So I married Layla's mom, Alison. She loved money." Remington shrugged, his blue eyes gazing out at the water. "The problem was, she didn't love *me*."

"Sorry about that." Owen took a long drag of his beer. He'd never really been into smoking pot before, but suddenly, he really wished he was stoned. He had a feeling this conversation would be much more tolerable with a huge joint.

"So we got divorced. And I dated a lot. And I'm telling you, man to man, I loved it. Hated my job, but loved the way women loved me." He jiggled his fishing line into the water. Suddenly, it jumped. "Aw yeah!" Remington yelled, and Owen could just imagine him scoring a touchdown in college. He quickly reeled the fish in. An ugly, brownish fish with steely-gray eyes flopped helplessly at the other end of the line.

"Dogfish." Remington shook his head ruefully. "These little fuckers latch onto anything put in front of them, especially if it's shiny. Can you hand me those gloves under the bench?"

Owen stood up and opened the top of the pine bench. He rummaged through until he found a pair of pine green rubber gloves.

"And, not only that, but their back fins can give you a gnarly rash if you're not careful," Remington explained as he carefully unhooked the fish and threw it back into the water. Owen could just make out its body quickly wriggling away under the surface.

"Anyway, what was I saying?" Remington asked, leaning back and taking a large sip of the rum punch that one of the boat's mates had brought up to him.

"Dogfish are poisonous and like shiny objects," Owen repeated. He knew he sounded like an asshole.

"Yes, exactly!" Remington said, as if proving a point. "And that was how it was with the women I was dating. They looked like they were catches, but they weren't. And then I realized, I didn't want to catch dogfish. I wanted to wait. Maybe that's why I gave up fishing," Remington mused. "Anyway, you've heard enough of this old guy's story. What about you? What are you fishing for in your life?"

Owen paused. In a totally wacked way, Remington's fish metaphor sort of reminded him of his own life. He was tired of hooking up with girls, then just moving on to the next. But Jack was different. He didn't know what she was thinking or what she wanted or if she even liked him. "I guess I'm still learning to identify the dogfish." Owen cracked a smile. Maybe it was the sun and the beers, but suddenly, shooting the shit with Remington didn't seem so bad.

Just then, Owen felt a strong tug on his reel. Remington stood up, throwing his own reel on the deck. "Okay, just pull in. I can steady you," he said as Owen struggled to control the suddenly heavy rod. Using all of his arm muscles, he attempted to twist the reel back as Remington held on to his elbow.

There, at the other end of his line, was a three-foot-long, pointy-nosed, gray-and-white fish.

"You caught a marlin!" Remington said, clearly impressed.

Owen grinned. That *was* pretty cool. Maybe this whole deep-sea fishing adventure wasn't as bad as he'd thought it would be. Maybe Remington wasn't so bad either.

Remington set to work taking the fish off the line. "That's what we all wait for. Our marlins. And you immediately know when you've caught one. And if you know what's good for you, you don't let it go," he said sagely.

Owen nodded. He wasn't sure if Remington was talking about girls or fish anymore, but it didn't matter. It was so clear now: Jack was a marlin. She was feisty and exotic and hard to keep up with.

And he's obviously fallen hook, line, and sinker.

"Tell you what," Remington said as a crewmember came over to take the fish. "I've already had a big wedding. I want this to be about our new family coming together. Invite a couple friends from New York. My G5's at Teterboro; they can be here tomorrow morning, and I'd love to meet your buddies"

"Really?" Owen grinned and took another gulp of his beer. Inviting all his friends down to the Bahamas was a pretty cool idea.

As long as he delivers a Hurricane Hugh warning to those who may need it . . .

a's certainly not getting married today

The walls of the Landing, the smallest and coziest of the resort's four restaurants, were covered in gauzy white material, making it feel like everyone was having dinner in a private tent. As soon as Chef Jean Luc had learned that Remington was getting married, he'd insisted on closing the Landing and catering a private rehearsal dinner for the family. Between his food and Yvette's exacting eye, they'd created an ultra-romantic evening.

Avery smiled in satisfaction as she drained her third glass of Veuve. She felt ridiculously happy sitting next to Rhys, her tan, bare shoulder just touching his Hugo Boss–suited one. Above her, she could just make out stars in the clear night sky through the gaps in the palapa-thatched roof.

At the head of the table, Remington and Edie were feeding bites of chocolate soufflé to each other. A steel-drum band played in the corner, making it almost impossible to hear anything. The long, rectangular table was dotted at intervals with orchid-filled Lalique vases, obstructing the view of the other side of the table.

Because of that, or because of the champagne, Avery turned

and boldly brushed her lips against Rhys's cheek. So *what* if Owen saw. What could he do?

"Are you sure? People can see us," Rhys whispered, squeezing Avery's hand tightly under the table.

Rhys's cell beeped loudly, just as the steel-drum band was finishing a reggae version of "Over the Rainbow." He quickly dug into his pocket. Just to be an asshole, Owen had changed his ringtone, so the song "Big Pimpin'" came on whenever he got a text from Hugh.

"That's a nice song!" Edie said, bopping her head to the ringtone, completely oblivious to the lyrics. Remington smiled fondly at his fiancé.

"Sorry, it's my phone," Rhys admitted, quickly snapping it to silent.

"So, do you think we should do performances tonight? Or tomorrow?" Edie said to the group.

Avery glanced up in horror. Her mom had this thing about making the guests at any of her parties do a performance after dinner, citing it as a Native American ritual. When she and Baby had been younger, they'd had to sing songs or recite poems together. Now she was really hoping they wouldn't have to participate.

Besides, she's already given her high-maintenance-bride performance today. . . .

"I think tomorrow might be better. During the reception," Avery murmured, making a mental note to speak to Yvette and make sure performances didn't happen.

"Good idea!" Edie nodded thoughtfully. "That way, all your friends will be here!" Edie clapped eagerly, then resumed feeding Remington bites of soufflé from her plate.

Avery shuddered. Remington had gotten the idea to fly some of their friends down tomorrow in his Gulfstream. She wasn't sure how many people were actually going to show up, but she'd invited Jiffy and Genevieve, and Rhys and Owen had invited some of the swim team guys. She certainly didn't want everyone to get an eyeful of weird performance art. But she was looking forward to showing off being a couple with Rhys.

A performance in its own right.

Avery lightly caressed Rhys's leg under the table. All her life, she had wanted just one thing: to find love. But even for all her dreaming, wishing, and hoping, she'd had no idea how *good* it could really be. Yesterday, Rhys had sent her cute messages first thing in the morning and last thing at night. He squeezed her hand or caressed her face at every opportunity—any sweet gesture to let her know he wanted to touch her but couldn't. And best of all were the times where they really *could* be together. He had sneaked into her room for a quick kiss before dinner, and her lips were still tingling from touching his. She couldn't wait to just tell Owen and make their relationship public, so that she could kiss him whenever she liked.

Rhys's phone beeped again, and he hastily pressed silent on his phone. In his excitement over coming to the Bahamas tomorrow, Hugh had outdone himself with texts. He didn't even want to *think* about what would happen when Hugh showed up in person.

"Dude, it's Rhys's mom," Owen teased, drunkenly holding up his champagne flute in a mock toast. He'd been in better spirits ever since his boat ride with Remington, and had been drinking and toasting their nuptials all night long.

"Oh, how sweet!" Edie cooed, clearly thrilled at the concept of Rhys being so close with his mom.

"I need to see what Lady Sterling says!" Avery said, grabbing Rhys's phone and flipping it open. She *loved* that one of the privileges of having a boyfriend was having carte blanche to their texts.

When I see you tomorrow, I expect a full report on your sexcapades. Not getting some is not an option.

Avery couldn't bring herself to read the rest of the text. She closed the phone, her heart dropping like it was in free fall. Was that what all this was about? Did Rhys just want to get laid?

Avery's head spun as she mentally reviewed the last few days, suddenly seeing everything in a new light. Rhys had flirted with her from the start, but when they hadn't so much as kissed, he'd gone to those pool skanks instead. She and Rhys had made out a few times—but clearly he wanted more. His provocative texts from the last few days didn't seem so *sweet* anymore. Even the way he had apologized to her the other day, telling her about his dream, seemed cheap now. He hadn't dreamed about them holding hands, skipping down the beach. He'd dreamed about them *hooking up*. Avery felt incredibly used. She'd been *played*.

Don't hate the player, hate the game.

"What the hell?" Her voice was icy and shaky, and she knew any second she'd burst into tears. She thrust the phone toward him. "That's what you're trying to do? I thought you were different." Avery stood up at the table, rage coursing through her veins.

"Oh dear," Edie murmured. She'd always ascribed to the hands-off parenting theory that it was better to let your kids work out their own problems and only offer input when they asked you. "Remington, we have a big day tomorrow, so let's retire to our villa. We should let the kids enjoy without us oldsters hanging around!" she announced, dragging Remington—who was still holding his plate of soufflé—after her.

"Avery, I need to explain. It's Hugh, it's the swim team, it's this—" Rhys went to grab her hand, but she shook him away. She pushed her chair back, ready to storm out.

"Avery?" Jack asked questioningly, standing as if ready to follow her out.

Avery ignored Rhys, turning toward Jack. Of course, Jack had nothing to do with this. But Rhys wasn't the only one who'd been a colossal jackass on this vacation, and Avery had had enough. "You're just like him," she spat, watching as Jack's green eyes went wide with shock. "A total fucking user, and a liar. You tell me you're here because you missed me, but really you just want my brother. And who knows what you've told *him*. You have a boyfriend, for fuck's sake!" Registering the shock on everyone's faces, Avery knew she'd done enough. "Just—everyone—leave me alone." She turned on her heel and marched out of the restaurant with her head held high.

Baby scraped her chair back, then paused. After all, wasn't she also lying and using the people around her? She hadn't spoken to Riley at all today, even though he was sitting just two seats down from her at the table. Yesterday, he'd made her feel on top of the world. Today, what they'd done had made her feel . . . confused. She still liked him, but she liked Layla. And Layla was her almost-sister. She pulled her chair back toward the table.

Rhys stood up, ready to run after her, ready to make her believe that the text wasn't what it sounded like. Because he knew how very bad it sounded.

"Don't even *think* about it," Owen hissed, practically pushing Rhys back onto the wicker chair. He couldn't *believe* his best friend had been hooking up with his *sister* behind his back. The fact that Rhys had lied to him about "not being over Kelsey" was just icing on the fucked-up cake. "You've done more than enough," he spat. Owen quickly ran outside to the marble patio, chasing after Avery.

Rhys sat back in his chair, watching helplessly as his best friend and his almost-girlfriend ran away. He couldn't believe he'd fucked things up with them *both* in one fell swoop.

Jack watched them go, too, feeling exactly the same way.

Misery loves company. . . .

tortured romance isn't as fun as it seems

"Yikes," Layla murmured, after Jack and Rhys had excused themselves, both looking shell-shocked. Only Layla, Baby, and Riley remained at the table.

"I hope they work it out before the wedding," Riley added unhelpfully.

"Yeah," Baby murmured, not really listening. She topped off her champagne. Baby didn't usually drink, but she couldn't deal with herself right now. She was terrible at not showing her emotions, so she'd avoided being in the same room as Layla as much as she could since their dinner last night. Luckily Layla seemed to have attributed Baby's odd behavior to having mixed feelings about the wedding, like Owen, who had thrown tantrums the whole trip before finally seeming to come around.

Baby took a long swig of her champagne, enjoying the hazy, floaty feeling as the bubbles coursed down her throat. She closed her eyes and wished that when she opened them, she'd be alone with Riley, in some fantasy land where his soon-to-be-ex-girlfriend wasn't becoming part of her immediate family tomorrow.

"Well, isn't there a saying, like, bad rehearsal dinner, good wedding?" Layla shrugged her shoulders as she glanced between Riley and Baby. "I mean, at least it's not your mom and my dad fighting!"

"True," Baby allowed. She was happy for her mom, and definitely didn't want anything to go wrong with the wedding tomorrow. But she couldn't help but think that if Remington were out of the picture, Layla would be too. "Baby, would you be okay if Riley and I go work on the music for our set?" Layla asked. She adjusted the sleeve of her blue American Apparel tunic dress and her tribal tattoo came into view. "I swear, this guy's been avoiding me"—she punched Riley playfully in the arm—"and we haven't worked out which songs we're going to do yet."

"Yeah, let's go work on the set, but let's wrap up early. . . ." Riley shot Baby a meaningful look. "I want to get a good night's *sleep*." Even though he was speaking to Layla, he didn't break eye contact with Baby the entire time.

Baby felt her stomach twist. He was inviting her over to his room later. And while there were a million reasons why it was wrong, just one glance at Riley's lopsided smile reminded Baby how *right* they'd been yesterday. Maybe they could hook up and then Layla would break up with him and she'd never have to know. After all, they were *practically* broken up. Layla had said as much yesterday. And after tomorrow, Riley would go back to Ithaca, and Baby wasn't sure when she'd get to see him again. It was just so confusing. She took another long sip of her champagne.

At least she's not confused about her feelings on drinking.

"You're okay, right?" Layla seemed hesitant to leave Baby alone, after the evening they'd all had.

"Yeah, I'm going to turn in early too," Baby said, speaking in code. She glanced away from Layla. After all, she wasn't doing anything *wrong*. After all, Riley wasn't hiding anything. He was sweet and sincere and didn't want to hurt his girlfriend. It was understandable. If she'd been a student at Ithaca and had met Riley in the dining hall or philosophy class or at some coffee shop in town and he'd given her the same explanation about his and Layla's relationship, she wouldn't have thought twice about hooking up with him.

Toto, we're not in Ithaca anymore. . . .

"You ready, Layla?" Not waiting for an answer, Riley stood up and walked out. But not before giving Baby a parting wink.

Even though his back was already turned, she couldn't help but wink back.

An hour later, Baby made her way back to the villas. She'd sat at the restaurant for a while alone, sipping champagne, listening to the steel-drum band, and sort of enjoying the feeling of being in such a complicated romance. At least, it had seemed hazily romantic, after she'd polished off all the champagne left at the table.

She crossed the villa's shared deck and made her way to the sliding door of the guys' villa, pushing it open gently. Baby tiptoed inside the room. The lights were off—Riley had probably kept them low so that if the boys came home, they'd think he was sleeping. She padded silently through the living room and gingerly opened the bedroom door. She could just make a figure curled up in bed. She moved toward Riley, when the figure moved and she saw that it was not one body but *two*. They were entangled, a bundle of writhing limbs. Through the sliver of the moonlight coming through the window, she could just make out a very feminine arm.

One with a tribal tattoo.

Baby turned and darted from the room, careful not to make a sound. She ran over to the deck outside the girls' villa and threw herself down onto one of the chaises. She felt like she was going to be sick and closed her eyes, hoping that the world would stop spinning.

Riley hadn't been waiting for her in his room.

He'd been hooking up with *Layla*.

Because she was his *girlfriend*.

Somehow, Baby's life had veered so far from where it had been just a week ago. She didn't cheat. She didn't believe guys when they swore to her they were about to break up with their girlfriends. And she certainly didn't get drunk and start crying about it. Tears ran down her face and she angrily wiped them away. She heard footsteps but didn't look up. She didn't want to talk to anyone.

"Hey." Jack's voice floated over to her.

"Hey." Baby didn't look up. Maybe if she ignored her, she'd go away.

Nice try.

She heard a chair scraping on the deck floor next to her, then Jack settling into the chair next to her.

Baby wiped her eyes with the back of her hand and stared at Jack. She was wearing a tight black dress and looked effortlessly beautiful, as usual. Other than Riley, she was pretty much the *last* person Baby wanted to see.

"Are you *crying*?" Jack asked. She pulled a Tiffany lighter from her bag and lit up a Merit. "Want to smoke?"

"No, I just think I need to be left alone," Baby said.

Jack exhaled smoke up into the night air. "Well, that's not an option," Jack said firmly. "I'm an expert in fucked-up drama, and your sister currently hates me, so just lay it on." She lit up another cigarette and passed it over to Baby.

Baby struggled to stand. Maybe if she crawled into the villa right now and fell asleep, in the morning it would all be better. Maybe when she woke up, she wouldn't be a wannabe boyfriend stealer. Or a traitorous stepsister. Or whatever she was.

"Well, at least sit down," Jack commanded.

Baby inhaled deeply on the cigarette. She'd never really liked smoking, and hated the burning sensation in her lungs now. But even though it didn't feel good, it sort of felt right, at least for the moment. It wasn't as if anything could get much worse.

"Thanks." Baby exhaled a cloud of smoke. She'd stopped crying and now her insides just felt numb. How could she have gotten so carried away? "I know we've never really talked, but I just wanted to say that I'm sorry about J.P." Baby pushed her long tangled brown hair back from her face, then pulled a few strands into her mouth. It was totally disgusting, but when she got super-nervous or upset, she always sucked on her hair.

"You need to apologize for *that*," Jack said, pushing Baby's hand away from her hair. "And why are you apologizing for J.P. *now*?"

"I hooked up with Riley," Baby confessed in a rush of words. It felt good to say it, even though Jack Laurent was the last person she'd imagined she'd be confessing to.

"You did?" Jack turned to her in disbelief. Her freckles looked even more prominent after a long day in the sun.

"I didn't mean to," Baby added. That didn't really sound much better. "You know, I'd never . . . when J.P. and I . . . we never hooked up until you guys had broken up." It felt good to tell Jack the truth. Still, it didn't change how awful she felt now.

"That's the past. We're talking about now. You hooked up with Riley," Jack replied matter-of-factly. Baby's hair was falling down her back, she was hugging her knees to her chest, and she looked like a miserable kindergartner who'd gotten sent to the corner for stealing someone's toys without asking. Had Baby *done* it with Riley? Or J.P.? Jack couldn't help but wonder.

"I know. It just happened. But I thought it meant something. And then I caught him with *Layla*," Baby said miserably. The last part came out almost as a whisper.

Jack sat up and looked Baby straight in the eye. "Look, I'm going to tell you what I think: You can't cry over someone else's boyfriend. They're *supposed* to hook up. They're *a couple*. But you're making a fool of her, sneaking behind her back. Honestly, I feel worse for her than I do for you."

"Thanks," Baby said sarcastically. "That really makes me feel great."

"You *shouldn't* feel great," Jack said seriously. "You need to tell her what happened. She needs to know. I'm telling you this for your own good." Jack drained the rest of the champagne glass. Part of her wanted to give Baby even more of a lecture, but she just couldn't. Even though it wasn't right, she could tell how upset Baby was about this. Plus, Baby was Owen's sister and Jack didn't want to alienate her. "You don't have to tell her *tonight*," Jack said, a little more softly.

Baby nodded. She couldn't believe it had to come from Jack, but the advice was completely right. She had to tell Layla. "I don't feel good," Baby said suddenly, this time for real. She could feel the champagne mixing with the caviar-rolled potatoes in her stomach. Whoever thought that combination was a good idea was a sadomasochistic moron. Baby stood up and ran into the girls' villa, straight to the bathroom.

Ew. If there was one thing Jack couldn't handle, it was puke. She'd had to deal with it at her father's house, when the step-brats had a bout of the flu, and absolutely didn't want to deal with Baby being a drunken mess. Still, she just couldn't leave her heaving and crying in the bathroom.

With a sigh, Jack stood up and followed her inside. Baby, shivering and even more disheveled than normal, huddled over the toilet.

"Hey." Jack knelt down, gingerly lifting the hem of her black Vena Cava dress so that it didn't touch the floor. She cautiously rubbed Baby's back until Baby's heaves subsided.

"There," Baby said when she finished, leaning away from the toilet. "That was gross, I'm sorry."

"It's okay." Jack stood up and ran a washcloth under the faucet, then passed it to Baby. "Are you feeling better?"

Baby nodded, then, surprisingly, her face broke into a smile. "Who knew you were so nice?" she teased.

Jack smiled back. "You owe me." She arched an eyebrow.

Suddenly, Baby laughed, then hiccupped. Jack laughed too. Maybe Baby Carlyle wasn't a boyfriend-stealing hippie skank. Or maybe she *was*, but was trying to change. In any case, it just felt good to finally let her guard down. "Come on," Jack said softly, "Let's get you to bed."

Twenty minutes later, Jack had taken off Baby's Havaiana flip-flops, force-fed her three glasses of water, and tucked her into bed. Now she was sitting on the wraparound deck, smoking a Merit and looking up at the stars. She could hear the waves crash against the shore. Even though the island was only a few hours' flight from New York, she felt very far away from her old life.

Jack still couldn't wrap her mind around the fact that Avery had lashed out at her like that at dinner—not that it wasn't warranted. Avery was right. Coming here, she had lied to just about everyone: to J.P., to Avery, even to herself. She didn't need a vacation. She didn't need to run away. She needed to take a long, hard look at her life and figure out exactly what it was she wanted.

One thing she definitely wanted was Owen. But she knew that he was out of the picture now. She hadn't seen his face when Avery announced that Jack was basically a scheming, lying ho-bag, but she knew he'd probably never look at her the same way again.

But, she realized, just because she couldn't have the guy she *did* want didn't mean she should keep around the guy she didn't. She had just told Baby to tell the truth, and face facts. Now, she had to do the same.

She pulled out her phone. Three missed calls. All from J.P. Not to mention eight texts.

Miss you, gorgeous.

Thinking of you.

You're my world—and I want you back in my city!

Jack used to be the type of girl who loved that kind of attention from a boyfriend. Now it just made her feel trapped and claustrophobic. She knew what she had to do.

She dialed 1, her speed dial for J.P., and held her breath as the phone rang and finally went to voice mail. She took a breath.

"We need to talk when I get back to New York." Jack choked back a sob, suddenly fully aware that this was it, there was no turning back, that maybe this was the *it*, the big moment she'd been preparing for all along. "Things . . . aren't working."

a's never been in love before

Avery sat on the white sand, gazing out into the ocean and wishing she could cry. She could cry at the dumbest things: a paper towel commercial on TV, getting a B on a chem assignment. But the trick was, she'd always feel the tears before they came and let them loose when she was by herself. It was one of the things she prided herself on: to never, *ever* cry in front of people. Now she was alone. But even though she just wanted to let everything out, she couldn't summon a tear. Instead, her heart just felt like lead.

"Ave?" She heard her brother's voice above the waves. It sounded like he was coming from the direction of the villas.

"Here," she said numbly, just so he wouldn't think she'd drowned or something.

"Oh, good." Owen jogged over. In the moonlight, she could just make out his blond curls flopping over his blue eyes. "Can I sit down?"

"If you want." Avery shrugged. She didn't really have any energy to argue.

Owen settled next to Avery, drawing a spiral in the white sand with his finger. The two siblings sat in silence for a while. Avery sort of wished she could tell him how she felt, but so much had changed since Nantucket. Even though they'd only lived in New York for three months, it felt like they'd become totally different people. They were still navigating how to relate to each other. "Why didn't you tell me you liked Rhys?"

"I was going to." Avery shrugged. "But it doesn't matter because all he wants to do is have sex." She spat out the last word.

"That's not true," Owen shook his head vehemently. He'd been pissed at Rhys when he'd first found out about him and Avery. His protective instincts had kicked into gear. But as he walked around the resort, looking for Avery, he'd had some time to think. Yeah, Rhys shouldn't have lied to him. But really, Rhys was only doing it for Owen's sake, because he didn't want him to get overprotective and mad. It was going to take a little time to get used to the idea of his buddy hooking up with his sister, but at the end of the day, Rhys was a good guy, and Owen knew that he shouldn't stand in the way.

"How *would* you know? It's all everyone wants," Avery squeaked. Finally, real tears started to flow. She was so sick of always having to think about who was hooking up with whom, who'd dated whom, who was planning to hook up with whom . . . why did it all come back to the same thing?

Darwin says: Because as a species we're hardwired to procreate.

"Avery, listen to me," Owen said gently. His sister looked up. Her black eye makeup was streaked around her eyes and her hair was wild around her shoulders. The last time Owen had seen Avery cry was probably when they were five and he'd accidentally hit her with a swing and knocked out her front tooth. Usually, Avery looked so put together. Now, she just looked like his sister who needed comforting.

Some lessons about the workings of the male mind wouldn't hurt, either.

"Listen, Rhys is great. It's not what you think," Owen explained. "The texts were sort of my fault. We had this dumb swim team idea that the only way Rhys would get over Kelsey was to hook up with a random girl. So I found these crazy, drunk British girls and was pushing them on Rhys. But it was just because I didn't know about you two."

Avery paused for a moment. "That's the lamest thing I've heard," she finally blurted. Owen saw the corners of her mouth twitch, like she was trying really hard not to smile.

"Lame? Don't overestimate us. It was idiotic. But, seriously, could I make that shit up?" Owen shook his head in bemusement.

Darwin says: Males are also hardwired to be idiots.

"I guess not." Avery sighed as she wiped her eyes with the back of her hand. "Still, maybe he's just not ready for a relationship."

"And maybe he is. You guys will have to work that out together."

"Have you ever been in love?" Avery asked curiously.

Owen thought again about Kelsey. He'd really thought he'd loved her at the time. He'd even stolen Avery's Frédéric Fekkai apple-scented misting spray from her shower because the smell had reminded him of Kelsey. But now he couldn't even really remember what it smelled like. Then he thought of Remington and their conversation on the boat. Remington had waited for years to find true love because he'd made the easy choices, dating women who didn't inspire or challenge him. Owen didn't want to be like that. Not now, and definitely not when he was Remington's age. Maybe he did need to calm down and stop playing the field or hauling up dogfish or whatever the right metaphor was.

"No," Owen finally confessed. "But if you fall in love with Rhys, you can tell me what it's like." He draped his arm around his sister's shoulder.

"Thanks." Avery sighed deeply. "But the whole thing just made me think—maybe we just got together because we were on vacation, you know?" She stood up and brushed off the back of her dress. "I don't want to think anymore tonight. Walk me back?"

"Of course," Owen said, taking his sister's arm.

Somebody's going to get the brother of the year award.

a certain british girl is hungry like the wolf

Rhys perched miserably on one of the tall bar stools surrounding the horseshoe-shaped bar in the center of the hotel lobby, oblivious to the couples enjoying drinks around him. He slid his empty glass toward the elderly bartender.

The bartender poured him another Scotch on the rocks. His third. "Be careful, buddy," the bartender warned, pushing it back toward him.

"Thanks," Rhys grunted. He picked up the drink and chugged the amber liquid, liking the way it burned his throat. Right now he could use the distraction. Nothing in his life made sense. Owen wanted to cut off his balls. Avery thought he was an asshole. But he wasn't an asshole—he was just a pussy. Why couldn't he have told Hugh to fuck off? Why couldn't he have told Owen the truth? He sighed angrily.

"Oi, Rhys!" Issy was eagerly making her way down the four steps that led into the sunken bar. She waved her arms wildly, her silver sequined dress riding up on her thighs. The other patrons looked over in amusement.

"Miss?" a hostess standing near the bottom of the staircase asked skeptically.

"Me mate's over there. That fizzin'-lookin' bloke with the brown 'air," Issy exclaimed indignantly.

"That your girlfriend? No wonder you're drinking!" the bartender whispered to Rhys as he moved down to the other end of the bar.

"You look buggered," Issy said, settling onto the stool next to Rhys and shaking her platinum blond hair out of her eyes.

"Er, hi," he mumbled.

"So, Elsie's off lookin' for your man. Where is he? You 'idin' 'im?" she asked as she gestured to the bartender. "Vodka with Diet Coke, please!"

Rhys cringed. Diet Coke and vodka? She totally *was* his cousin's wife Nicola. "So, I thought we'd all 'ave a bit of a laugh yesterday—then you all skivved off, like. Did you find some other bird?" She sat on the very edge of her stool so that their knees were touching.

"What?" Rhys hissed. She was talking too fast, her accent too strong for him to understand.

Issy sighed, then turned toward him and locked eyes with his. "Did. You. Shag. A. Girl?" she asked slowly, as if Rhys were a three-year-old.

"Oh, er, no," he said, turning back to his drink. No, he most definitely did not.

"'Ere now," Issy said, putting her hand on Rhys's thigh. "You seem pretty cut up about something. You all right, love? You can talk to me."

Rhys looked at Issy. She was wearing a large silver nameplate necklace that read ISOBEL in rhinestone letters. Her silver eye makeup matched her dress, and he could just make out her dirty blond roots. She'd be pretty if she didn't try so hard. But mostly, she sounded nice. And Rhys needed a friend right now.

A friend with benefits?

He drank the rest of his Scotch for some liquid courage. "Let's talk somewhere quieter." Maybe he should just get the stupid pact over with. At least then he wouldn't feel like a loser tomorrow, when all the swim team guys got here.

"There's a good lad." Issy leaned in toward Rhys and kissed him. He could feel her fake acrylic fingernails on his neck, and her mouth tasted like cigarettes and Red Bull. Still, he wasn't about to be picky. He kissed her back.

Rhys heard footsteps behind him, but he didn't care. So what if they got kicked out of the bar? They could just go to her room and get it over with. Then maybe he could fall asleep and everything would be better tomorrow.

He felt a tap on his shoulder.

"I'm busy," Rhys hissed, even though he instantly knew who was behind him. Why was Owen butting in, after basically telling him they weren't friends anymore? Rhys turned back to Issy. But Owen wouldn't let go of his shoulder.

"Sorry, he needs to go," Owen explained to Issy, pulling her off Rhys.

"No need to get all stroppy. We were just gettin' to know each other, just bein' all friendly like," she protested, pouting as she stood up. "And by the way, mate, Elsie's looking for you. You're a right man to just blank her like that," Issy said indignantly, straightening the strap of her dress that had fallen down her shoulder. "Now, where were we, love?" She sat down on Rhys's lap.

"Dude, we have to go," Owen said, moving closer to Rhys. There was urgency in his blue eyes. "I know you like Avery. She's your marlin."

And Issy's no catch.

Rhys tore his eyes away from Issy's exposed cleavage and stared up at his friend. It was as if hearing the name Avery turned on a sober switch in his mind. Even if no other part of Owen's sentence made sense.

"She likes you. I mean, she *liked* you, before she thought you were like a pimp or something. But you won't have any chance with her if you don't come with me now," Owen said sternly.

That was all Rhys needed to hear. Even if he only had a *chance* with Avery, that was enough. And if this meant Owen was okay with it . . .

Rhys practically shoved Issy off his lap and drunkenly followed Owen out of the bar and to the golf cart parked outside.

Way to make a clean getaway.

gossipgirl.net

hey people!

Texting during calc. Skipping a week of school to ski in Switzerland. Eating endless desserts at Payard. Why is it that when something is forbidden—by our teachers, by our parents, by ourselves—we just want to do it that much more? And what happens when formerly forbidden things get a stamp of approval? Either you become totally debaucherous—hello, gross twenty-first birthday parties where people act like they've never drunk before—or the activity totally loses its appeal. (Remember when you were six, and all you wanted to do was cross the street by yourself? Now, wouldn't you just rather be driven everywhere via town car?)

The same applies to love. If you're faced with the choice of going out with a guy whose mom is *your* mom's best friend, or a smoldering stranger who's barely allowed in your building because of his shaggy hair and bad boy rocker look, is it any question who you'd choose? They say the heart wants what it wants, but I'd like to add a layer to that: The heart also wants what it can't have.

your mail

 Chère Gossip Girl,
So, I am living in New York and going to school here and I met a darling American boy and had hoped that we'd spend this weekend of thanks together in his town house, but today he just informed me he is heading on an unexpected tropical island getaway and is not bringing me. What to do?
—tragique

Dear T,

Sadly, it seems you may have been this guy's belle de jour. My advice: Take a tropical vacation of your own.

—GG

sightings

H and a bevy of St. Jude's swim team boys, getting in a town car and heading toward **Teterboro** airport. Out of the pool and into the ocean? **J** and **G**, racing through the swimsuit section at **Barneys**—last-minute shopping? Hurry, or you'll miss the plane! . . . A sad-looking **J.P.**, all by himself watching a matinee of *The Umbrellas of Cherbourg* at the **Paris Theater** in Midtown. **S** and an elderly, pearl-wearing lady getting matching tattoos at some gross place on St. Mark's. Talk about cross-generational bonding!

You know you love me,

gossip girl

love is all around

Avery awoke to what sounded like rain. She'd been having a dream that she was a princess who sent messages in bottles to find her prince, but the only guys who responded were Abraham Lincoln, Owen's gross friend Hugh from the swim team, and Jim the grandfatherly doorman. It had really disturbed her. She sat up and rubbed the sleep out of her eyes. They felt puffy and she briefly worried about what she'd look like tomorrow during the wedding.

Doesn't she mean today?

She heard another sound. It didn't sound like rain anymore; it sounded more like someone knocking on the door. But, glancing at the clock, it was only 5 a.m. What the hell?

Avery swung her feet onto the cool stone floor and padded over to the sliding door. It was probably just Layla coming back from the guys' villa or something. But, glancing at Layla's bed, Avery could just make out her stepsister-to-be, sleeping fitfully. Weird.

Avery opened the door to see only a note, written on the white resort paper in jagged black pen.

Look under your bed.

Avery went back to her bed and gingerly knelt down, her beige Cosabella mid-thigh-length silk negligee skimming the floor. She hoped this wasn't a practical joke by Owen. She knew he'd probably want to make her feel better, but she simply was *not* in the mood. She picked up the bed skirt, and, in the semi-darkness, could just make out a picnic basket with a bottle of champagne sticking out. She pulled it out and into the sitting room, where she turned on the lights. There was another piece of notebook paper.

If this is better than a monster, come outside.

She grinned and ran to the door, not even bothering to change into something more appropriate or put down the picnic basket. There, standing in the shadows, was Rhys. He was wearing khaki shorts and one of Owen's Nantucket Pirates T-shirts and looked like he hadn't slept at all. He smiled shyly as he saw Avery.

"I had Layla sneak that under your bed. I'm so glad you're here."

"Hi," Avery said. She didn't know what else to say. She shivered as the surprisingly cool breeze hit her skin.

"Here." Rhys held out a large maroon St. Jude's swim team sweatshirt like a peace offering. "In case you're cold. I thought we could have a picnic and watch the sunrise. You know, before the craziness today."

As if it could be any crazier than yesterday?

"Right." Avery nodded. She wondered if this was still a dream. But Rhys's strong hand on her shoulder felt very real to her. They walked together in silence, toward the beach.

"You know, I want to apologize," he said finally as they reached the sand, where the sun was just starting to come up.

"I know. I talked to Owen," Avery said. After their talk last night, she'd come to bed and stared up at the ceiling, thinking it all over. She knew she'd overreacted—with Rhys, and with Jack. And she felt badly about that. But she also knew she'd reacted so strongly for a reason. "I shouldn't have run off like that. I got carried away. It's just—I like you," Avery said in a rush of words. She stared straight ahead at the white beach, which seemed almost illuminated. On the horizon, she saw the slightest sliver of light.

"I like you too," Rhys said shyly. He stood in front of Avery so that she couldn't look anywhere else. And then, not bothering to set down a blanket, he pulled her down onto the sand and kissed her.

And they lived sappily ever after.

does b believe in something that she's never seen before?

Baby adjusted the straps of her bridesmaid dress and frowned at her reflection in the mirror on the bedroom doorway. The dress, which Avery had picked out, had a scoop back that was sexy without being slutty, and was a deep purple color that looked surprisingly good on everyone. Baby liked the short length, which showed off her newly tan legs. Still, she had a low-grade headache from last night and was dreading seeing Layla. After her talk with Jack, she knew she had to tell her the truth. While it wasn't exactly going to be fun, she had to let Layla know that her boyfriend was going around telling people they were about to break up and making out with said people and basically breaking their hearts. Not that she was bitter or anything.

Of course not.

"Do you need me to zip you?" Layla asked as she walked in, wearing the same dress as Baby. She'd just had her hair done in the other room, which had been taken over by the resort's salon and transformed from villa sitting room to something resembling John Barrett's at Bergdorf's. Her curly blond hair was loose, with four or five tiny braids holding an orchid in place and giving just the right touch of hippie-elegance to her look. Her tribal tattoo was visible, and she looked comfortable and confident.

"I'm good," Baby said as she twisted to pull the zipper into place. "Actually, I need to talk to you." Baby settled on the bed, not worrying if her dress would get wrinkled, even though Avery would kill her if it did. She felt like she was in an updated version of *Cinderella*, except somehow, she'd landed the wicked stepsister role.

Which is at least better than the wicked witch role.

Layla sat down next to her and nodded. "Totally. I've had a lot on my mind too, seeing my dad and your mom together. It's just made me think, you know?" Her green eyes suddenly got a faraway expression, before they snapped back to Baby. "I'm sorry, I'm totally interrupting. You go first!"

"No, you go," Baby managed to croak. She knew she was delaying the inevitable, but she needed a second to collect herself.

"Okay, well, don't tell anyone, because I'm not going to do it until after the wedding." Layla chewed her bottom lip thoughtfully. "I'm breaking up with Riley."

"What?" Baby was speechless.

"Don't say it like that!" Layla held up a hand. "I feel like everyone will say that. I mean, we've been together forever, you know? We started a freaking *band* together. But, honestly, we're not in love." Layla shook her head. "I mean, your mom's weird and my dad's a total freak. But together, they *fit*. It's not easy like that with Riley. It's the opposite, actually. It's always just so *hard*." Layla sighed.

"But you guys seemed very . . . *together* last night," Baby said before she could stop herself. She blushed. Not wanting to reveal that she'd been in Riley's room, she backpedaled. "I mean, you didn't come home last night, so I figured—"

"Breakup sex," Layla said matter-of-factly. The topic didn't make her blush in the slightest. She looked down, playing with the hem of her floaty purple dress, before drawing her eyes back up to Baby. "But as nice as it was to fall asleep in his arms, when I woke up there early this morning, knowing I had to go get ready for my dad's *wedding*, it was like, what am I *doing*? I know Riley's not right for me in the long run. I know we can't keep this relationship up. So why drag it out, you know?"

Baby slowly nodded, not sure what to say. So Riley had been telling the truth. And now, it seemed, the relationship had taken its natural course. Of course she still knew that she'd done something wrong. Of course she wished things hadn't happened the way they had. But she also felt like a great weight had been lifted off her shoulders . . . and she also felt a glimmer of hope. Riley would be single soon. Maybe, after an appropriate period of time . . .

"Baby, you have your hair appointment now!" Avery marched in, breaking the quiet mood. She was holding a clipboard and looked beautiful, with her hair pulled back behind her ears, one orchid attached with a jeweled butterfly-shaped brooch to hold it in place. It would be so easy to keep everything that happened with Riley to herself. After all, Layla would never know. But then she'd always have this secret. Forever.

"Thanks," Baby said to her sister. "I need a few minutes."

Avery frowned but backed off upon seeing Baby's determined expression. "If you're sure . . . but five minutes." She trailed off and turned on her heel into the bedroom.

"What's up?" Layla asked, confusion in her eyes.

"Look, I know you might hate me after I tell you this . . . but you need to know. Riley and I kissed on Friday. It was before you and I talked and I wanted to tell you, but I didn't want you to be mad," Baby said in a rush of words. She looked down at her neatly lilac-polished fingernails. They looked like someone else's hands. Just as her confession felt like someone else's. "I'm sorry," she added desperately. She felt tears beginning to well up.

"That day you and Riley went riding," Layla said slowly.

Bab nodded miserably. "We kissed. It just . . . happened," Baby added, hating the way the phrase echoed in her ears. It didn't just happen, not really. It had happened because Riley was cute and interesting and he'd be the type of guy Baby would have loved to have gotten together with in another time or place.

Layla sighed slowly. "It's okay."

Baby glanced up at Layla. Her mouth was set in a firm, hard line.

"I mean, I wish you had told me earlier, but it's not really a surprise. I had seen you and Riley flirting that first day. Maybe I needed to see him flirt with another girl to make it clear that we've moved on from each other," Layla mused.

"I'm really sorry," Baby said again. "I knew it was wrong, and I wanted to tell you, but I was just afraid you'd never talk to me again. I'm just . . ." She trailed off, and then looked Layla in her green eyes. "I'm just really glad you're going to be my sister."

Layla's face broke into a genuine smile. "I guess I'm certainly getting a crash course in sibling relations this trip."

Just then, Avery burst back into the room. "Baby, come on," she demanded, almost tapping her foot,

"It's okay," Layla said, standing up. "Hug?"

Baby nodded, then threw her arms around her stepsister-to-be's skinny frame. "Thank you," she murmured into her hair. "Thank you for being my big sister."

Layla smiled back. "Anytime. And hopefully, after today, a lot of the time."

Finally, Avery had succeeded in herding the family down to the beach. The wedding party was accompanied by Hamish, a kilt-wearing Brooklyn performance artist friend of Edie and Remington's who'd just arrived on Shelter Cay that morning and who was serving as their officiant.

Because nothing says official like a kilt.

Remington and Edie's procession took them from the villa steps to the beach as Riley and Layla sang a surprisingly sweet version of the Peter, Paul, and Mary song "(Wedding Song) There Is Love." Folk music was never going to be Avery's thing, but she had to give them props for trying. She still couldn't believe she'd managed to get everyone dressed and all in the same place at once, but here they all were.

"Everyone here, then?" Hamish asked, his back facing the ocean.

In front of him stood Remington, looking handsome in a seersucker suit. Edie stood beside her husband-to-be, wearing the Ralph Lauren dress. Avery had been right—it was perfect on her, making her look young, vibrant, and naturally beautiful, a younger version of Meryl Streep from the movie *Mamma Mia!*

Minus the singing. For now.

"All right then," Hamish announced, yelling over the sound of the waves.

"Actually, let's all stand in a circle!" Edie bellowed. "Better energy. What I'm thinking is sort of a May Day pagan ritual

scene," she explained, as if she were an avant-garde theater director. Avery grinned, suddenly finding her mom's over-the-top
ideas endearing. The confused group slowly sorted itself into a
circle. Rhys was standing next to Avery, and she squeezed his
hand. He squeezed hers right back.

On the other side of the circle stood Baby and Layla, fingers linked in a show of sisterly solidarity. Jack and Owen stood
next to each other, and Owen was smiling at Remington and his
mom. Riley, not part of the wedding party, was standing with the
crowd of fifty-plus people—word had spread at the resort that
an impromptu wedding was taking place, and suddenly everyone
was invited—gathered on the beach.

"Love is all around," Hamish announced grandly. "Edie and
Remington are two people who don't need permission for anything. So who am I to tell them what to do? You're married, you
can kiss whomever you want!" he announced.

Short and sweet.

Edie grinned. "Remington, I love you!" she said, standing on
tiptoe to kiss him. Avery threw her arms around Rhys's neck.
Baby and Layla hugged each other tightly.

"All right, time to have fun!" Edie announced brightly. "Remington, let's race!" She tossed her bouquet of orchids behind her
and skipped up the limestone beach steps, Remington following
her, a ridiculously cheesy grin on his face.

As the wedding party made its way to the villa complex, where
the reception was being held, Baby felt a light touch on her arm.
She turned to see Riley, looking adorable in a pair of khakis and
a white linen button-up, the top button undone and his dark hair
tousled from the beach breeze.

"Hey," he said, his dark eyes scanning hers. "Congratulations," he added, leaning in to kiss her on the cheek. Baby wasn't sure if you were supposed to congratulate the daughter of the bride, but her cheek tingled where his lips had brushed it.

"Thanks," she said, being careful to walk a foot away from Riley, even though their bodies seemed to pull toward each other with a force of their own. "I guess they really did it," Baby said, smiling at her mom's retreating back, Remington's arm drawn around her small waist.

"I guess they did," Riley said with a boyish grin. "And speaking of people making things happen . . ." He trailed off, and Baby had a feeling she knew what was coming. "I'd really like to see you again. Ithaca's not exactly close to the city or anything, but I come in some weekends. Maybe we could get coffee sometime?" He gazed at Baby. His tone was hopeful, and yet she could tell he was sure she was going to say yes.

Baby looked straight ahead as she mulled it over. Two days ago—two hours ago, even—she'd dreamed of this exact scenario: Riley and Layla breaking up, of their own accord. Baby having the chance to see Riley again, guilt-free. But as she glanced over at Layla, who was saying something to Avery, her head thrown back in laughter, a new sensation came over her. It wasn't guilt. It wasn't lust. It was just . . . caring. She cared about Layla, and about her new family. She was starting to think that Layla might be the more important relationship to foster here.

Baby turned back to Riley. "Thanks," she said, and he grinned, probably already planning their next rendezvous. "But no thanks," she finished. She gave him a final, lingering kiss on the cheek, and made her way over to her sisters.

everything comes out in the wash

Avery grinned in satisfaction as she surveyed the villa complex. Yvette and her team had worked around the clock last night to surround the pool with white lights and gauzy white tents. Food was piled everywhere, and guests mingled with tropical drinks in their hands. Avery recognized a couple of the swim team guys as well as a couple of her mom's weird artist friends, who were currently sitting by the side of the pool, engaged in a spontaneous drum circle.

"This is terrific," Rhys said as he walked over to Avery from the bar, carrying two icy glasses of rum punch. "*You're* terrific."

Avery smiled as they made their way over to a small cluster of guys from the swim team. Genevieve and Jiffy hadn't come. They'd missed the last trip that Remington's Gulfstream had made this morning—apparently due to Genevieve's need for a last-minute bikini—and had texted saying congratulations and that they'd see her at school this week. Avery knew she should be disappointed that she wouldn't have the chance to show off Rhys to everybody. But she found that she really didn't care.

"So, you're saying you perform nude? That sounds great,"

Hugh Moore said loudly from a few feet away, where he was in the midst of a conversation with one of Edie's yoga-toned performance artist friends.

"Hugh's making friends already." Rhys shook his head. "See what I was dealing with?" Avery squeezed Rhys's hand. She was *so* glad he wasn't like that.

Remington clapped his arm around Avery's back. He was holding Edie's hand as if afraid to let go. "You did a great job planning this." Avery smiled. She'd never seen her mom so vibrant and happy.

"And to think, we've been waiting for over twenty years to do this," Edie murmured.

"I'd have waited another twenty!" Remington roared.

Rhys cleared his throat. "Congratulations, sir!" he announced, holding out his hand.

"Thanks, son!" Remington shook his hand. "Oh good Lord, it looks like Susan is resurrecting her nude performance art." He frowned over in Hugh's general direction. "I'll put a stop to that. After all, we're not twenty anymore!" He laughed.

Avery quickly looked away, since she *really* didn't want to see Hugh's attempt at performance art. She saw Jack coming from the bar, two glasses of champagne in her hand.

"Hey," Jack called. "I brought you a drink. Oh, you have one," she noted as she got closer. "Can I borrow Avery for a second?" she asked Rhys.

"I'll be back," Avery murmured, letting her fingers brush against his. She wasn't mad at Jack, not anymore. But she should probably tell *her* that.

They made their way through milling guests and waiters over to the small wood gazebo that overlooked the ocean. Avery sat down on the glider swing in the center, pushing it back and forth with her foot. "I'm sorry I was sort of a bitch last night," she said finally.

"One of us has to be. That's kind of how we're friends, right?" Jack said with a wry smile. She settled next to her on the swing.

"True," Avery allowed. She took one of the glasses of champagne. It was weird how she and Jack could go from enemies to friends and back again. Still, it felt right.

"I broke up with J.P.," Jack said finally.

"Oh." Avery wasn't sure what else to say. Now it seemed Jack and Owen were free to date. Well, good. Avery didn't know why she'd been so bent out of shape about it before—maybe it was just the idea of her friend and her brother having fun without her. The idea that they didn't need her. But really, she just wanted everyone to be as happy as she was. "So, you want to go out with Owen?" Avery asked, a mischievous smile playing on her lips.

Jack blushed, gazing down at her ecru Calvin Klein sheath dress. "Would you be mad if I did?" she asked, her pretty face twisted in concern.

"You don't need my permission. If you like him, tell him!" Avery pronounced, downing the rest of her champagne. Love had made her more generous than ever.

"Thanks," Jack said, and by the look in her green eyes, she meant it. "Now, you have to get back to *your* guy," she added, half-sternly.

"I know, I should have told you, but—"

"No details!" Jack held up a manicured hand. "Just go for it."

After Avery left, Jack sat for a couple more minutes on the swing, watching as the other revelers ate, drank, laughed, and enjoyed the cool Caribbean breeze. It was a magical night, and Jack was just glad to be a part of it. Still, there was one thing missing. She wanted to talk to Owen, maybe even tell him how she felt, if he didn't know already. Thinking about it made her stomach flip-flop. It was strange and scary and wasn't easy. And Jack liked things to be easy.

In fact, she preferred things to be as easy as pulling out her black AmEx.

She stood up and headed over to the bar. She'd have one more glass of champagne and think through exactly what to say.

Beside her stood a super-skinny blond girl wearing what appeared to be a red latex dress that hit mid-thigh. Next to her was a brunette wearing far too much gold jewelry. Jack stared at them, trying to figure out how she knew them. And then it hit her: They were the girls she'd seen talking to Owen and Rhys the day she'd first arrived. Jack had actually been jealous of them at the time. How long ago *that* seemed now.

Almost instantly Hugh, one of Owen's lame swim team friends, sidled up to the girls.

Directed by skank sonar?

"My fair ladies." Hugh leered at the two girls as he stroked his full blond beard lasciviously. "Might I say you look lovely?"

"It's true, innit," the blond girl said as she elbowed her friend, giggling. Jack rolled her eyes, glad these three soul mates had found each other, when she felt someone come up beside her.

"I have an idea," Owen whispered as his arm gently brushed hers. Jack's heart thumped wildly just at the sight of his deep blue eyes and adorable white-blond hair. Owen nodded at Hugh and the two girls. "What do you say we make this a pool party?" he asked, a devilish grin on his face. "I'll be in charge of Hugh— you're in charge of them." He raised an eyebrow at Jack.

Jack stared. One of the girls teetered just inches from the

edge on her unstable, glittering heels. It was almost too easy. She didn't really know why they were doing this, but Jack wasn't one to choose decorum over fun. Especially not when Owen was the one offering.

Who would?

"Fine!" In one moment, she shoved the blond girl in, while Owen pushed Hugh. The two of them flopped messily into the water with a huge splash. The brunette girl, not knowing what else to do, shrugged and jumped in after them.

"Everybody get in the pool!" she cried as soon as she touched down, her drink still in hand. In an instant, her red dress was floating on the top of the water as she, Hugh, and the blond girl splashed each other in the shallow end.

"That was kind of dumb," Jack admitted, even though secretly it was the most fun she'd had all night.

"Yeah, but at least now we can't hear them." Owen grinned.

Jack stared at Owen's tanned, happy face, glad to see him smiling—especially at her. So did this mean he didn't think she was a scheming would-be cheater? "I broke up with J.P. I just wanted you to know," she blurted. It wasn't exactly how she'd planned on telling him, but then, nothing this week had gone as she'd planned.

"Oh?" Owen looked surprised. And, Jack hoped, a little pleased.

"Yeah." She shrugged. She didn't want to think about what would happen next or what it would be like when they got back to New York. This was still her vacation, at least for tonight, and she wanted to have fun. "Want to go swimming?" Not waiting for an answer, she dove in, still wearing her dress, enjoying the heavy feel of the now-ruined silk around her body.

"I'm coming in too!" Baby appeared by the side of the pool, her brown curls bouncing wildly around her pretty face. She slid off her flip-flops and did a perfect swan dive into the pool, splashing Jack.

"Bitch!" Jack yelled good-naturedly, splashing Baby right back.

"Remy, let's jump in!" Edie called from the other end of the pool. There, she carefully slid in feetfirst, still in her wedding dress.

Avery shook her head at the ridiculous scene—of course her mother's beach-chic wedding had turned into one giant pool party, seventh-grade style. The thing was, it looked *fun*. She glanced at Rhys, her eyes wide with excitement.

"I'll jump if you jump," she said, already kicking off her Christian Louboutin slingbacks. Rhys grinned right back.

"Miss Carlyle?" Avery felt a pointy finger tapping her shoulder. She whirled around to see Yvette, the wedding planner. Her skinny, angular face was pinched and she looked like she was about to have a heart attack. "I can assure you, this is *not* what I was expecting when we were discussing the party details. This is not typical."

"Sorry." Avery shrugged. "This family isn't typical." She jumped in, making sure to splash Yvette and her pink Chanel suit. Rhys cannonballed in next and swam up to her. He was shirtless, but still wearing his dress pants. He pushed Avery's hair out of her eyes.

"Fireworks!" Someone yelled at the other end of the pool. Avery looked up. The night sky was splashed with reds and blues. But instead she looked into Rhys's brown eyes and kissed him.

It may have taken sixteen years of waiting, but it looks like somebody finally found her prince.

gossipgirl.net

Disclaimer: All the real names of places, people, and events have been altered or abbreviated to protect the innocent. Namely, me.

| topics | sightings | your e-mail | post a question |

hey people!

In honor of the hippie-tastic wedding of the century, please forgive me while I quote some Bob Dylan and say, the times they are a changin'. Who'd have thought the triplets' bohemian, anything-goes mom would actually get *married*? Certainly not the Sunday Styles section, whose editor was so surprised that the paper crashed an announcement into this weekend's edition—complete with a photo of the pool-soaked wedding party. Can't wait to see what **A** will do when she sees that . . . unless she's learned by now that infamy is better than anonymity. With her track record, she should have!

The Shakespearean comedies all end happily: with a wedding. Because really, what's more promising than love? We all like to turn up our noses and pretend to be cheesed out, but the promise of a happily-ever-after gets everyone . . . including me. So bask in the glory of this happy day, and enjoy the fairy-tale ending. But don't get too comfortable. Because I'm *always* watching.

See you back in Manhattan!

You know you love me,

gossip girl

Blair Waldorf, Serena van der Woodsen,

Nate Archibald, Dan Humphrey, and

Vanessa Abrams went off to live their lives.

Now, they're coming home for the holidays.

A lot can change in a few months . . .

but some things never do.

Turn the page for a sneak peek of

I will always love you

a new gossip girl hardcover
featuring the original cast

gossipgirl.net

Hey people!

The more things change, the more they stay the same.

For years, New York City—the center of the universe, the place where anything can happen—was our home. But we've moved beyond our uniform-required, single sex schools and into bastions of higher education around the country. Yes, it finally happened: We went to college. For the past few months, we've been surrounded by people who don't know whom we've hooked up with, who don't remember the time we wet our pants on the playground in kindergarten. We've learned new things and made new friends and maybe even met the loves our lives. We've changed.

Or at least, *some* of us have. Others are just as fabulous as always. Take **B**, heading to Vermont to spend a perfect holiday with her perfect Yale boyfriend and his perfect family. That girl always had her eye on the prize. . . . And speaking of prizes, what's rumored SAG nominee **S** doing these days? Formerly worshipped by her Constance Billard class-mates, she's now followed by paparazzi and a posse of fellow movie starlets. No matter where she is or what she does, **S** will *always* be the center of attention.

Then there are the people who've tried their hardest to change: **N** is on a sailing trip around the world. But as we all know from reading Kant in our freshman seminars, no man is an island. He'll be back. Then there's **D**, scratching out poetry in his Moleskine notebook in the Pacific Northwest. It may look like a total lifestyle change, but he still insists on Folgers instead of French press in the coffee capital of the US. He also spends every waking moment attempting to Skype his shaven-headed, ultra independent filmmaker girlfriend, **V**, who's at NYU and seems to almost . . . have *hair*. And friends. Lastly there's **C**, last seen with a pack of flannel-wearing, very rugged boys. Is he into a new type, or has he gone through yet another reinvention? That man puts Madonna to shame.

Everyone's back in town for the holidays, and this winter break is guaranteed to be filled with makeups, breakups, and shakeups. Lucky for you, I'm going to report *everything* worth reporting. Let the reunion begin.

sightings

B on a train from New Haven to Montpelier, VT, looking very out of place in a sea of flannel . . . **S** with three identical girls, on the red carpet for a premiere. . . . **V** and some friends from NYU, including her very young, very cute teaching assistant, at a film-screening party in Bushwick. Is someone trying to get extra credit? . . . **D** and his little sister, **J**, splitting a plate of chocolate-chip pancakes at one of those curiously packed diners on upper Broadway. . . . **C** and a group of cowboy-boot clad guys ordering sodas at the lounge at the **Tribeca Star**. Ride 'em, cowboy!

break the rules

Remember, you don't technically live under your parents' roof anymore. You've already indulged them in holiday merry-making: Scrabble with the siblings, kissing Grandma, and decorating cookies that nobody's going to eat. Which means now is the time to use all your pent-up energy to party. Remember, you can always reform after January 1—that's what resolutions are for. So go out, have fun, and most of all, show your former besties and former flames just how much *better* you've become.

Besides, now that you know I'm watching, aren't you just dying to put on a show? Thought so.

You know you love me,

all *b* wants for christmas

"You awake, Scout?"

Blair Waldorf awoke from a nap to the sight of her boyfriend, Pete Carlson, gazing down at her. Pete smiled his adorable, lopsided smile. His eyes were a yellowish brown and reminded Blair of her cat, Kitty Minky.

She threw the plaid Black Watch duvet to the foot of the couch and discreetly checked for drool with her index finger. She *loved* being woken up by Pete, especially when he called her by an adorable nickname. Currently, it was Scout because she'd directed him and his three older brothers to the best Douglas fir Christmas tree, deep in the woods of the Carlsons' expansive Woodstock, Vermont, estate.

"Of course I am," Blair lied, sitting up and yawning. Why sleep when her waking life was so much *better*?

"Good." Pete settled next to her on the couch, pushing Blair's long bangs tenderly off her small, foxlike face. Her hair was a little shaggier than she'd like, but she simply didn't trust any of the hair salons in New Haven. Besides, what were unkempt bangs when she was with a guy who loved her?

"Have any dreams? You were making these little growls in your sleep. It was cute." Pete pulled the blanket off the floor and draped it over their legs.

"Oh." Blair frowned. She was *growling*?

In truth, she'd been having a lot of weird dreams lately. Last night, she'd woken up and thought she was at a sleepover at her old best friend Serena van der Woodsen's house, only to find herself all alone in the guest bedroom of the Carlsons'.

Maybe it was just homesickness. After all, she hadn't seen Serena since August, she didn't have a home in New York anymore, and no one in her family was even in the United States this week. Her father, Harold, was celebrating Christmas in France with his boyfriend and their adopted twins. Her step-brother Aaron was spending the break on a kibbutz in Israel. Her mother, stepfather, brother Tyler, and baby sister Yale had moved to LA back in August, to a gigantic, tacky Pacific Palisades mansion that they were making even bigger and more tacky. While the renovations were taking place, they were spending the holidays in the South Pacific, visiting the islands that Eleanor Rose, in a fit of pregnancy-induced mania last spring, had bought for each member of the family. Blair had been somewhat tempted to tag along, if only to see her baby sister, the least fucked-up member of her tragically absurd family.

Not to mention pay a visit to Blair Island.

But once she'd been invited to spend Christmas with the Carlsons, she felt it was her duty as a girlfriend to go.

"I was just dreaming about you. Us. I'm just so happy." Blair sighed contentedly as she gazed into the orange fire roaring in the wood-burning stove across the room. Outside, a thin blanket of snow covered the ground.

"Me too." Pete ruffled her hair and pulled her face into his for a kiss.

"You taste nice," Blair breathed, letting her body relax into Pete's muscular arms.

It was funny how things worked out. When she arrived at Yale, Blair discovered that her roommate, Alana Hoffman, sang a cappella all the time. Blair would wake up to Alana singing "Son of a Preacher Man" to her collection of teddy bears. Avoiding her room, Blair spent a lot of time in the library, where Pete was writing a paper for his Magical Realism in the Caribbean class. They'd exchanged flirty glances, and finally Pete invited her for coffee.

It was amazing how *easy* everything could be with Pete. For the first time in Blair's nineteen years, her life felt like it made sense. She loved her classes, had an adoring, handsome boyfriend, and had even found a surrogate family in the Carlsons.

For the past few days, they'd spent every waking hour with the family: his former US senator dad, Chappy; his Boston debutante mom, Jane; his three older brothers, their wives, and assorted nephews and nieces Blair couldn't even try to keep straight. It sounded like a nightmare, but it was great. His dad was barrel-chested and red-faced and told bad jokes in a way that made everyone crack up, and his mom would randomly recite poetry at the dinner table without being drunk. The brothers were friendly and smart, their wives were nice, and even the kids were polite. So far, it had been a perfect holiday.

And it was about to get even better. To celebrate the New Year, Chappy had booked the entire family at an exclusive resort in Costa Rica. Obviously, Blair could do without the rainforest adventure part, but she'd heard the beaches were pristine, the sun was hot, and the villas had the most incredible mattresses.

Just then, there was a knock at the door. "You kids decent?" Pete's brother Jason called as he entered. He had the same lanky frame as Pete. Tall, blond, and handsome, all four of the Carlson brothers—Everett, Randy, Jason, and Pete—looked like they could be quadruplets, even though there was a two-year age difference between each of them. A second-year law student at UPenn, Jason was the second youngest of the Carlson brothers. He was adorable, and Blair would've had a crush on him if she wasn't dating Pete.

At least she has a backup.

"We're playing charades. Your presence has been requested."

"Do we have to?" Blair suppressed a groan. It was cute in theory, but they'd played charades, Pictionary, or Scrabble the last three nights.

Maybe they should shake it up with some truth or dare.

"And guess who's requested you on his team again?" Jason smirked, flashing Blair the trademark white-toothed Carlson smile. "Our dad loves you!"

"Aw, that's cute!" Blair said, mustering her enthusiasm. They'd be at the resort soon, so she might as well continue being as polite and friendly as possible to his family. She followed Pete through the wide, arching hallway that led to the kitchen. A large wood stove hunkered in the corner opposite two massive Sub-Zero refrigerators. Several overstuffed yellow chairs sat in front of a large dormer window, each one containing a different member of the family. Pete's father Chappy stood in front of the group.

"Scout!" He called happily as he spotted Blair and Pete.

"Hi, Mr. Carlson." Blair smiled warmly.

"I already claimed you, so back off, boys," Chappy said jovially to Pete's brothers, who all smiled politely back at her. "I'm telling you, Scout, I don't know how I'm going to manage without you next week," Chappy continued.

"Oh, well, I'm sure we can play on the beach or something," Blair said. She blushed. "Play charades on the beach," she clarified.

"Yeah, but what'll I do without my favorite teammate?" Chappy shook his head sorrowfully. "No offense, Jane." He cupped his hand over Blair's ear. "My wife cheats," he whispered, winking at his wife. Jane Carlson had wheat-blond hair cut in a sensible bob and was tall, with an athletic frame. Only the deep wrinkles in her forehead made her seem old enough to be Pete's mom, and they didn't make her look ancient so much as friendly.

"I do cheat, I'll be the first to admit it," Jane said merrily. "I'm glad you're on the straight and narrow." She winked at Blair.

But Blair was still stuck on the part of Chappy's sentence that implied she *wouldn't* be in Costa Rica with them. She'd bought five new Eres bikinis for the occasion. They made the most of the five pounds she'd gained from Yale's meal plan. "*Without me?*" Blair repeated stupidly.

"I mean, I'd bring you along, but we've got a saying in the Carlson family . . ." Chappy began, his eyes shining, as if he were about to deliver a stump speech. "I believe, when it comes to vacations, in the *no ring, no bring* rule."

"It's the Carlson curse." Jason sighed, elbowing Blair in the ribs sympathetically. Blair stepped away. While it was true she'd never *officially* been invited to Costa Rica, she'd been invited for Christmas, for God's sake. Wasn't that even more exclusive than a beach holiday? And why *not* invite her? After all, she'd brought Nate Archibald, her high school boyfriend, on her family vacations for years and it wasn't like she'd been married to him.

Except in her dreams.

"Blair, we love you and we want you in our family for years to come, but I need to be a stickler on this," Chappy explained sympathetically, as if she were one of his constituents, arguing over some impossible and arcane rule. "I've raised four boys, and while they've behaved around you, honestly, these gentlemen cause more theatrics when it comes to ladies than the Yale School of Drama," he finished.

"Maybe you could get together with your girlfriends and have a girls' adventure!" Pete's sister-in-law Sarah piped up from the corner of the room, stroking her eight-months-pregnant belly. "I remember when I heard the Carlson rule, I had a great time with the Theta girls. We went to Cancún!" A look of happy reminiscence crossed Sarah's heart-shaped face.

"You did?" Randy asked, shooting a look at Sarah. "I didn't know that."

"All I'm saying is that Blair should have her own fun." Sarah winked conspiratorially at Blair.

"More hot chocolate, anyone?" Pete's mother asked, excusing herself.

"Sorry, son!" Chappy said, genuinely sounding remorseful as he clapped Pete on the back. "Sorry, Scout!"

Blair narrowed her eyes at a painting that hung over the fireplace, of a ship in what looked like an exceptionally violent storm. What type of fucking art was that to hang in a house? And what the fuck was up with that stupid nickname? Scout?

Out would have been more appropriate.

"Blair, I'm sorry," Pete said simply. "I thought you understood . . ."

"What? I knew I wasn't coming," Blair lied, smiling fakely. Her stomach was churning wildly. For a brief second, she wanted to excuse herself, run to the second-floor bathroom, and puke everything she'd eaten for the past five days. But she didn't.

"Blair, darling, here's your hot chocolate. I made sure to put some extra marshmallows in there." Jane pushed the steaming mug into Blair's hands. "Won't you sit down?" She gestured to one of the comfortable overstuffed chairs.

"Thanks," Blair said. She squared her shoulders and turned to the waiting Carlson clan. "You all ready to play?" She forced herself to smile, a plan already forming.

"Maybe I *will* have a wild girls' weekend," she whispered to Pete. "I haven't been to New York all year." His face fell as he no doubt pictured all the fun she'd be having without him. Blair raised an eyebrow challengingly. After all, she was a woman. A Yale woman. She had places to go.

And games to play.

make new friends, but keep the old . . .

"This came from the man at the other end of the bar," the skinny bartender slash model said as he proffered a glass of champagne.

"Thanks." Serena van der Woodsen glanced down the long, dark oak bar of Saucebox, the new lounge in the just-opened hotel on Thompson Street. Breckin O'Dell, an actor she vaguely remembered meeting a few times, held up his own glass of champagne and saluted her. Serena nodded, brought the glass to her lips, and took a sip, even though she preferred vodka.

"Oh my God, you should totally date him. His agent has ridiculous connections," Amanda Atkins said, pulling on the sleeve of Serena's The Row scoop-neck jersey dress in excitement. "Can we get some shots down here?" she called to the bartender. Serena smiled indulgently. Amanda was an eighteen-year-old recent LA transplant best known for her role in a dorky sitcom about a girl from Paris who moves to a farm in Tennessee to live with her redneck uncle. Recently, though, she'd been cast in an indie film and was trying to break free from her good girl reputation.

Another shot and she's almost there.

"Maybe," Serena said unconvincingly. She stared at the bubbles fizzing to the top of her glass as if they held the secrets to the universe. If she looked around her, she'd see tons of Breckin O'Dell look-alikes, no doubt wishing *they'd* been the ones to buy Serena van der Woodsen—*the* Serena van der Woodsen—a drink. Instead, they buzzed around Amanda and her other two actress-friends, Alysia and Alison. They called themselves the three A's, even though Alysia's name was actually Jennifer.

The three A's were admittedly a little shallow, but they were also goofy and fun and never turned down a party. Usually, Serena had a blast hanging out with them, but tonight, she felt a little . . . off. Her parents had just left for St. Barts, while her brother, Eric, was spending the winter break in Australia with a girl who'd been a visiting student at Brown last year. It wasn't like she wanted to spend New Year's Eve with her family, but she also didn't like waking up in their huge Fifth Avenue apartment alone. Serena downed her champagne in one gulp, telling herself that she just needed to have fun.

And, after all, she is the expert.

"Hey, you're that farm chick!" one guy stuttered, not looking Amanda in the eye. His hair was gelled and he was wearing a pink and white striped button-down. It was clear that he'd had to bribe the bouncer to get into the bar.

"Yes," Amanda sighed. "But, actually, I have to stand over here now." Amanda took two steps away, as Alysia and Alison snorted in laughter. Serena offered the guy a sympathetic smile. Even though she was beautiful, Serena was never mean.

An infuriating combination.

"God, you'd think Knowledge would know to not let guys like that in. Did you see his hair? It was, like, sprayed on." Amanda flipped her extensions over her shoulder as she named the beefy bouncer whose job was to keep Saucebox as exclusive as possible, even though, to Serena, it felt exactly the same as every other bar she'd been to recently.

"Serena?"

Serena whirled around, ready to have another one of those *so great to see you* conversations with someone she'd probably met once. Instead, she saw a familiar, smiling face that immediately took her back in time.

"Oh my God, Iz!" Serena squealed excitedly. She slid off the smooth bar stool and threw her arms around Isabel Coates, a fellow Constance Billard alum who'd gone to Rollins College down in Florida. She was super tan and had highlights in her shoulder-length blond hair. She automatically looked over Isabel's shoulder, sure she'd see Kati Farkas, Isabel's best friend and constant sidekick. Isabel and Kati had done everything together back in high school. Kati even turned down admission to Princeton so they wouldn't have to be separated. But instead of Kati, a girl with a ski-jump nose and straight brown hair stood next to Isabel.

"This is my girlfriend, Casey," Isabel announced proudly.

"Oh." Wait, did that mean *girlfriend* girlfriend? Serena noticed Isabel's hand intertwined with Casey's.

"We met in a women's studies class." Isabel smiled adoringly at Casey.

There's her answer.

"This is Serena van der Woodsen. We went to school together," she explained.

"Nice to meet you, Casey," Serena said, holding out her hand to the tall girl, who took it gingerly.

"Nice to meet you too. I haven't seen any of your movies," Casey announced self-importantly.

"How's Kati?" Serena asked.

Isabel sighed and shook her head. "She has this, like, football player boyfriend and is pledging a sorority that wears pink sweatsuits to class. It's awful." She sighed disdainfully. "Casey and I pretty much do our own thing. But what about *you?* I saw your movie. You were pretty good," Isabel allowed.

"Thanks," Serena said, resisting the urge to roll her eyes. "Things are okay. Just working a lot. We're filming a sequel to *Breakfast at Fred's* that's coming out this summer, so that's fun . . ." Serena trailed off. Even though she'd been on the cover of the October issue of *Vanity Fair*, part of her felt stuck. After all, she'd come home from her big premiere to her same pink childhood bedroom in her family's sprawling penthouse. If possible, she almost felt *less* grown up than she had last year, especially since she now had an agent and a publicist who told her exactly what to wear, what to say, and who to be seen with.

"Sounds great!" Isabel cooed. "Anyway, I was just showing Casey all the old places we used to go. Remember how we used to, like, spend hours trying things on at Barneys? I just can't believe we were ever so *young*. Things have changed a lot," she mused, nuzzling her blond-highlighted head against Casey.

"Things *have* changed," Serena agreed. Less than a year ago, she and Blair and Kati and Isabel would meet before school to smoke Merits on the Met steps and imagine their lives in college. Now, Blair was a poli-sci major at Yale, Isabel was a lesbian, Kati was a sorority girl, and Serena was a movie star.

"So, have you seen anyone?" Isabel asked.

"No." Serena shook her head. For her, only two people really mattered: Blair and Nate. She and Blair had tried to keep in touch, and once Serena had sent Blair a package full of Wolford stockings and black and white cookies in a Barneys bag—all of Blair's favorite New York things. Blair had reciprocated with a stuffed bulldog wearing a Yale T-shirt. They'd send occasional e-mails and texts, but never anything long or involved. It was fine, though. Blair and Serena were the type of friends who could go weeks without speaking, then pick up right where they left off.

As for Nate . . . they hadn't talked since he left, to sail the world for a year. Serena wondered if she'd ever see him again. But she didn't want to think about that right now.

Or ever.

"Are you going to Chuck's New Year's party tomorrow night?" Isabel asked, draining the rest of her drink. "I mean, I know he's, like, such a misogynist, but I figured, you can only protest so much, you know? I prepared Casey."

"Wait, didn't Chuck go to military school?" She hadn't

thought about Chuck—with his sketchy history, his trade-mark monogrammed scarf, or his questionable sexuality—for months. But the last she'd heard, after getting rejected from all twelve schools he'd applied to, he'd gone to some underground, in-the-middle-of-nowhere academy. Of course her parents saw Chuck's parents socially, but they never mentioned him. It was an unspoken rule on the Upper East Side that parents didn't discuss their unsuccessful children.

"Who knows?" Isabel shrugged. "The party's on, though. I saw Laura Salmon at City Bakery this morning and she told me she spoke to Rain Hofstetter at some lame Constance alum tea party that Mrs. M organized. Thank God I missed that. But, anyway, I guess she talked to Chuck? I don't know. It's at the Tribeca Star. But I guess since you're a movie star and all, you probably have to host some MTV special or something, right?"

"Well . . ." Serena trailed off. In truth, she already had an invite to a party at Thaddeus Russell's Chelsea loft. Thaddeus had been her *Breakfast at Fred's* costar and was a true friend. But he wouldn't mind if she stopped by to say hi and then went off to Chuck's party.

"I'll be there," Serena chirped. She suddenly couldn't wait for New Year's Eve. How could she *not* go see her old high school crowd? While she may not have been thinking of them all that much recently, it wasn't like she'd forgotten them.

And they certainly haven't forgotten her.

I will always love you

a gossip girl novel

The secret is out 11.3.09